Love on Separate Grounds

Christiana T. Moronfolu

COVER DESIGN BY

Tolic Arts, Baton Of Love Ventures
batonoflove_ventures@yahoo.com

Print information available on the last page.

ISBN: 978-1-4907-9046-6 (sc)
ISBN: 978-1-4907-9047-3 (e)

Trafford rev. 08/22/2018

 www.trafford.com
North America & international
toll-free: 1 888 232 4444 (USA & Canada)
fax: 812 355 4082

Dedication

To my God and defender, of a truth your goodness and mercies do not fail. Your love is of immeasurable greatness and in your friendship, we find true love. People love for different reasons, some for good causes and others for alternative causes. This God is our God. When He loves you, you win in every sphere and on all grounds.

To my family and friends from the diverse cultures and works of life, though we may be on separate grounds or operate from separate grounds, remember there is only one genuine love. It's the love that satisfies. It's the God's kind of love. It's the love that delivers.

The Weapons of Love

The Weapons Of Love
Are Needed
In Your Onward Journey
From The First Breathe
Till You Breath Your Last
You Must Thus Be Guarded
With The Weapons of Love

The Weapons Of Love
Are Needed
In This Battle For Life
Where It's like A Board Game
In The Maker's Eye
You Must Thus Be Guarded
With The Weapons Of Love

The Weapons Of Love
Are Needed
Do You Know Them Too
They're The Ones That's Needed
When The Fight Is Nigh
You Must Thus Be Guarded
With The Weapons Of Love

The Weapons Of Love
Are Needed
Come And Take A Look
In The Gallery Of Love,
Winners Take Them All
You Must Thus Be Guarded
With The Weapons Of Love

LOVE ON SEPARATE GROUNDS

The Weapons Of Love
Are Needed
You Must Take Them All
The Order Doesn't Count
Finance, Fame, Friends And Foe.
You Must Thus Be Guarded
With The Weapons Of Love

The Weapons Of Love
Are Needed
In This Battle For Life
Losers Descend The Stairs
With Each Passing Second
You Must Thus Be Guarded
With The Weapons Of Love

The Weapons Of Love
Are Needed
In This Game Of Life
Play To Win Not One But All.
Finance, Fame, Friends And Foe
You Must Thus Be Guarded
With The Weapons Of Love

Chapter One

SANDAL OF LOVE

She had just finished her National Youth Service program in Abuja, where she had served as a teacher in Bright Mind Montessory Private School. Through the help and influence of her cousin; Olufayosimilokan Tolulope; often referred to as Fay, she was able to secure a visiting permit for six months. The twenty six years old Fay had come to Nigeria to get married to her thirty years old husband, Gbekeloluwa Olufeyinsimi and Ewaoluwa had been one of the bridesmaids. Having heard of her cousin's outstanding academic achievements and management skills, Fay had invited her over. The sky was the limit for Ewaoluwa Tolulope, so the stage was set to receive her cast.

On arrival in UK, Ewaoluwa lived with Fay and her husband in Sutton. She met and befriended few friends of the newly wedded couple and related well with them. She also attended quite a number of social functions. While the couple was out at work, she made herself useful by helping with domestic chores around the house. She also volunteered in various roles within their local church.

By her second month in UK, she met and fell in love with a thirty years old Indian man, Singh Ghandi who was a friend to Gbekeloluwa. Singh also worked with him in his internet café and sold computer parts and products. Fay had been confident that Ewaoluwa's skills would be beneficial to her husband's computer training program at the internet café. After her arrival, she had invited Singh over to the house. On visiting the couple, he sounded so friendly and chatty that he captured the twenty five years old Ewaoluwa's attention. He came across to her like an ideal man with his good looks and well groomed body features. They kept exchanging looks and smiles as he chatted away.

At the end of his visit, he took her number and invited her for lunch the next day and she accepted. Singh had openly declared himself as a single and available man searching for a life partner and Ewaoluwa felt it was an open invitation that was too good to miss. She fantasized about having a relationship with him throughout the night and it felt like she had just put on a sandal that was crafted in love, tailor made for her and which guaranteed a victorious walk into the garden of romance and freedom in the UK. She smiled as she slept off.

LOVE ON SEPARATE GROUNDS

The next morning, she woke up still flirting with the idea of having a relationship with Singh. She had admired his transparent and confrontational approach to the relationship and was clear about what he wanted. She hoped to find protection, comfort and marital covering. She had seen Fay's lifestyle and had coveted it from the first day she stepped into her home. Prior to that, she had been in regular touch with her cousin, who had told her so much about life in the UK. It was only natural for Ewaoluwa to desire living in the UK and she felt that Singh might be the one to fulfil the dream.

On their first date, she made him aware that she didn't believe in sex before marriage and he acknowledged her concerns and took her to the Bluebells pub Hackbridge. As they sat and drank some majaritas in the bar, Singh handed her a small bouquet of dianthus pink lases already set in a decorative Indian bowl and she thanked him. She was tall, pretty and had dark skin. She had well cut out manicured fingernails and toenails and wore a smart hair do. She wore a neat top and a smart pair of jeans and her pair of sandals was very nice. She had good etiquette too. Saturday, 1st June 2002.

Firstly, Singh asked about her family and she smiled and said they were all well. He smiled back and told Ewaoluwa about his relationship with his family and friends and how much they had influenced him. He was born in India, but his parents; Ajay and Sadguna were posted to Birmingham when he was about five years old. Ajay was a retired vetenary doctor while Sadguna was a home maker. It was said that when their home collapsed in India during a natural disaster, Ajay's entire family was killed in their hut, only baby Ajay escaped. He was found under a pile of rubbles after two days and his extended family named him Ajay, meaning the one who is invincible. He had been invincible to the powers of death. Ewaoluwa smiled and nodded in admiration but kept quiet.

Singh continued his story. His mother, Sadguna on the other hand came from a humble and wealthy family, where the ladies were thought to be very homely and submissive to their husbands. Her parents said that they wanted to call their children by the character they wanted to see in them so they named her Sadguna meaning good virtues. She later married Ajay and had four boys, Singh was the first. At infancy, the doctors in India thought he wouldn't survive childhood because he was born at seven months, with a number of complications. He beat the odds in the incubator and his father named him Singh meaning lion or a fighter.

Ajay and Sadguna had three other boys when they came to England and their joy of being in the western world inspired them to name their sons after light. They claimed they got the opportunity to be more enlightened in UK. Back in India, they had lived in the remote town of Spiti Valley. The town of Birmingham was the exact opposite; it was bustling with activities. Singh's brothers were named Aditya (sun or beginning), Arush (first rays of the sun) and Reyansh (a ray of light). Aditya was a vet just like his father in Manchester, Arush was a project manager in Blackburn and Reyansh was a builder in Birmingham. Although Ajay and his wife were delighted to be in Birmingham, they missed the breath taking views of Spiti and always spoke about the place while the boys were growing up. They were now retired and were contemplating relocating back to Spiti.

Ewaoluwa was so amazed at the family's apparent success and Singh's level of openness endeared him further to her. She made up her mind to hold onto Singh, as she was sure to find the love and comfort she so desperately crave for in marriage. With Singh, she was guaranteed a covering that would enable her reach her maximum potential in UK. He was the perfect walking aid she needed to get to where she wanted. In response, she thanked him for his story and told him how much she admired his family from the little that he had told her.

She then went on to shed light on her family. Ewaoluwa told him that she took so much pride in her family too. Her mother, Temiloluwa (mine is God's) had been friends with her father, Temidire Tolulope for almost twenty years.

LOVE ON SEPARATE GROUNDS

Temidire (meaning 'mine turned out well') had dated Temiloluwa for two years initially, and when they discovered that their blood genotype was AS, they decided not to get married but remain friends. They had first hand experiences of sickle cell cases in their immediate families and didn't want to go through it themselves by having children with sickle cell. Both decided to remain friends, encouraging each other but dating other partners. They dated several partners but there was no marriage.

Eventually after being friends for almost twenty years, in their mid forties, they decided to get married and be life companions. The Forty five years old Temiloluwa soon took in after marriage and had a beautiful baby girl with blood genotype AA. The Tolulope couple were so thrilled that they gave their baby girl the name 'Ewaoluwa', meaning the beauty of God. The couple felt Ewaoluwa was a lesson from God. She would have come earlier if the couple had faith and didn't avoid each other for so long. She had two other children at forty seven and forty nine respectively; Ileriayo (meaning 'the promise of joy') and Iriolusesimi (God's dew fell on me). Ileriayo's blood group was AS while Iriolusesimi had the sickle cell genotype SS. The Tolulope family now had to trust God that Iriolusesimi would survive the sickness. This made them give Ewaoluwa the nick name 'teacher' to remind them of God's lessons.

LOVE ON SEPARATE GROUNDS

More so the medical doctors assured the family that there was advanced research going on in the field and there had been a huge break through for SS patients. While they were growing up, the Nigerian medical research unit had discovered a drug that could drastically reduce Iriolusesimi's pains when she had crisis; the only side effect was that she had to sleep for longer periods, than the recommended sleeping hours. They also spoke on the possibilities of her getting a bone marrow transplant which was a more permanent corrective measure. This was expensive but the family trusted God for divine provision.

The three sisters attended Little Saints Infant and High Schools. Ewaoluwa's sisters graduated at Yaba College of Technology with Ileriayo graduating as a facilities manager and Iriolusesimi graduating as an interior decorator. They both married and settled in Abuja through their father's influence and soon teamed up and began to work together. Ewaoluwa was an exceptionally brilliant scholar and went onto the university to read education as her first degree.

Though she performed very well in academics, she was also very troublesome. The people around them attributed the level of her stubbornness to the fact that her parents were never around while they were growing up. She learnt to defend herself and her siblings from a very tender age.

LOVE ON SEPARATE GROUNDS

Ewaoluwa and her siblings were left in the care of Fay's father, Moboluwayo Tolulope. He and his daughter lived with them when his wife passed away at child birth. At her death, Temidire had comforted his brother. He reminded him of the meaning of his name Moboluwayo; it meant I rejoice with God. He encouraged him not to weep but see his baby daughter as another form of joy God sent to the family. They named the baby girl Olufayosimilokan meaning God put joy in my heart. She was fair and very beautiful.

Temidire was a truck driver, shuttling between Lagos and Abuja to deliver goods and Temiloluwa was a nurse in Surulere Health Centre. Both of them were hardly ever around due to the demands of their jobs. While Moboluwayo played the father figure in the absence of Temidire, the little family teacher Ewaoluwa played the mother figure in the absence of Temiloluwa. The Tolulope couple eventually split up when they couldn't make time out for their marriage.

After the split, Temidire relocated to Abuja with his brother Moboluwayo Tolulope and his daughter, Fay. They lived with him until they departed for UK when Fay gained admission to study for her A-levels. Temiloluwa continued with her job as a nurse and worked tirelessly as a nurse to ensure there was enough provision in the house to take care of the basic needs of her daughters. Ewaoluwa continued to look after her siblings.

LOVE ON SEPARATE GROUNDS

While at Little Saints Infant School Surulere, at age five, she had a body statue of a fat nine year old, her voice was deep and she bullied her peers and seniors. To encourage and control her, the teachers put her in charge of the class. At Little Saints High School Surulere, she continued bullying her friends and fighting. On one occasion in her fifth year, she beat up her mate, who called a group of young girls to gang up and beat her up. Her friends tried to intervene and a riot broke out, and she was eventually suspended from the school. Despite her truancy, she returned to write her final college exams and performed excellently well. She had the overall best result in the school.

As she grew older, she became calmer because she had more responsibilities that forced her to make optimum use of her resources. She had to work and study simultaneously because her father stopped assisting the family financially when he left them. On his brother's departure to UK, he moved in with another woman in Kuje area of Abuja. In the University, in her free time, she attended a couple of social outings. Although she was robust, tall and pretty, she never had any suitors because of her masculine approach to life and reputation as a trouble maker. All her dating attempts failed.

Singh held her palms affectionately as he heard the sadness in her voice. He told her that he found her story very impressive and courageous and her company very interesting. He also told her that she depicted an epitome of tenacity and fortitude. She responded by thanking him and said that she admired his humour and interest in people. He replied and said that he was interested in settling down with her in marriage and would want her to feel appreciated and loved. He also said he felt loved and respected by her offer to come out for a drink with him. He hoped she would feel the same towards him. She thanked him for being open and she also expressed her hope that the relationship would provide them with the love and warmth that would lead to a fruitful union.

Finally he took her back to her cousin's flat in Sutton and went to his home which was fifteen minutes away. Ewaoluwa continued to fantasize about Singh and how she would cling onto him as a sandal is fastened to the feet and walk on the grounds that would pave the way for her as she ventured into the world of romance. She was thrilled, for the first time; she had met someone who told her that he found her attractive and romantic. Singh had said that he wanted to marry her.

While she was growing up, her contending and competitive personality had kept most men away. She liked Singh from their first outing together and she hoped that they would be compatible. What helped their first date was the fact that they were both attracted to each another and she believed that the chemistry between them should lubricate the relationship and act as a binding force.

Over the next couple of weeks, Singh proved to be very caring, loving and interested in building friendship, loyalty and trust with her. She was determined to live up to his expectations. Ewaoluwa also learnt of Singh's previous relationship. He had gone out with Sabrina for about a year before splitting up. He attributed the split to personality incompatibility. Sabrina was a very jovial lady but she lacked focus and stability. Singh on the other hand was very sociable but focused and stable. He had tried to help her, but it was a drain on him emotionally and psychologically. She felt that he was too pushful and decided it was best to part ways. The relationship had ended amicably and it was a mutual agreement to part ways.

However, a month into their relationship, Ewaoluwa started complaining that she felt Fay and her husband were enslaving her. She prevailed over Singh, and they began to plan her escape to the city, where they would get decent jobs and be independent. Singh also vowed to protect their love, so Ewaoluwa could be free and comfortable.

Chapter Two

BREAST PLATE OF LOVE

In the fourth month of Ewaoluwa's arrival, during the October 2002 bank holiday, Fay and Gbekeloluwa decided to go for a week end break in Woolacombe Bay, Devon, to mark his thirtieth birthday. He had told Fay that he was particularly grateful to God and felt like marking the occasion. He was a love child and his mother had given birth to him in UK while she was in abject poverty. She was going to have an abortion quietely but the christian influence around her taught her to have implicit trust in God. She did and God met her needs and that of her baby. She named him Mogbekeloluwa meaning that I put my trust in God. She raised him single handedly and had to trust God for divine provision till he started working at sixteen years of age.

The Olufeyinsimi couple invited Ewaoluwa and Singh to Devon but both declined the invite on the premise that they had other engagements in Birmingham. The couple left for Devon without

LOVE ON SEPARATE GROUNDS

Ewaoluwa and Singh. Before they returned, Singh had found another job as a manager in The Lion Bar in Covent Garden. He had also helped Ewaoluwa secure a job as a teaching assistant with Smart Juniors School Kentish Town. They both rented a one bedroom flat within a terraced duplex close to the school. They had kept everyone around them in the dark as Singh became her defensive armour in UK.

On their return, Fay and her husband discovered that Ewaoluwa had packed her things and left. She left a note to apologise for not giving them enough notice of her departure. She said that she was sorry she had to abandon them but explained that she and Singh had decided to marry quietely in the registry. From there they would go to Spiti for their honeymoon and also help Singh's parents settle down. She advised them that they shouldn't expect her back as she felt it was time to leave and was indeed sorry to leave. She had found her protective cover.

Singh also left a note to say that he was terminating his work in the internet café run by Gbekeloluwa. The Oluwafehinsimi couple were shocked and disappointed; Fay hadn't expected the betrayal from Ewaoluwa. Her friends and family had accepted Ewaoluwa and Singh as couples and were looking forward to their wedding. It ended up being a disappointing end to a beautiful relationship between the cousins. Both Fay and her husband chose to ignore the behaviour of Singh and Ewaoluwa and move on with their lives.

The Kentish Town flat Singh and Ewaoluwa moved to was sited in a well landscaped environment and their neighbours had friendly cats and dogs. Ewaoluwa decorated the place with plants, animals, antiques, posters and wall decors. Ewaoluwa encouraged Singh to get to the registry, as she believed that they couldn't continue living together without getting married. Singh was so well behaved that he never slept with her; he remembered she told him that she didn't believe in sex before marriage.

Convent Garden was a very lively place so Singh and Ewaoluwa spent their evenings at the social venues there, when he wasn't working. Ewaoluwa quickly learnt the ropes of Smart Juniors School where she taught and within months, she was promoted to being a class teacher. She worked very hard at encouraging the children to talk freely but discouraging the use of cursing, swearing and negative words or words of despair. She encouraged thoughtful speech and mindfulness too. She was good at leaving a lasting impression on the children and their parents. She was never bashful or arrogant; she was always courteous and respectful. She made all parents feel accepted and welcomed to the school. Everyone like her.

LOVE ON SEPARATE GROUNDS

They had a very quiet registry wedding in Birmingham on Saturday 26th October 2002 and Singh's family and few friends were present. Their honeymoon was in Arun Indian Retreat by the Isle of Sheppey. Ewaoluwa couldn't believe how fortunate she had been in her entire life. Up till that moment, the only negative things that happened to her were her parents' divorce and her suspension from High School. Singh loved the beach and preferred to spend most of the time there. When it was bedtime, they retreated to their hotel room. As they went about their foreplay, Ewaoluwa discovered that Singh had pennisless syndrome. She was devastated and looked at him in disbelief.

He bowed his head and looked away from her as he reminded her that he had told her about it on their social outing. He had been born prematurely with a rare condition called bladder exstrophy, which led to the pennisless condition. She was startled again and as she opened her mouth to talk, no words came out. Her mouth was dry and she felt her legs faint. He continued to bow his head and keep quiet. She then summoned up courage to ask with some tremor in her voice 'err…. so does that mean that we can't have any baby'? He told her that they could still have a pleasant evening and enjoy their honey moon.

She asked him again 'Honey cut the chase; does it mean we can't have any children'? Singh sat down and grabbed a glass of cold water. He then went on to lecture her on how it was possible to have a corrective surgery, but nothing was certain. He told her that he wasn't concerned and won't consider the procedure because it was very expensive, it was time consuming and he didn't think it was worth the pain or money. She became totally devastated. She also sat on the chair next to him, her heart was palpitating.

She then realised that the mistake she made while they were courting was that she didn't carry out full investigation on the health condition he had mentioned. He told her that he had survived it and she had assumed all was well. She then pleaded with him to consider corrective surgery and his response was that he would think about it. They spent the night with Singh using his techniques. Ewaoluwa being a virgin felt fulfilled and satisfied, but was in total shock and disbelief as she tried to digest what she had just discovered of her newly wedded husband.

The week long honey moon soon came to and end and they were back in their Kentish Town flat. As she settled down to work and life with Singh, she constantly persuaded him to begin the process for the corrective procedure; he finally got angry and told her never to mention it to him again. He told her that she was free to leave if she wasn't satisfied with the marriage.

LOVE ON SEPARATE GROUNDS

On hearing that, she began to sink into depression. That meant she may not have any baby with him and the knowledge created some anxiety for her, which made Singh drift away. Their social outings together also reduced and Singh spent more time at work than at home. The piece of armour plate she thought protected her suddenly became non functional.

Apart from her teaching responsibilities, Ewaoluwa was made to do all the domestic duties in the home while Singh only came home to sleep at night. When he wasn't working, he came home briefly, had a wash and went out without stating where he was going. After a while, she became disinterested in the home and only focused on the school. Two years after going to the registry, Singh knew Ewaoluwa desperately wanted children and so he felt insecure when she hung around men in the clubs and bars or when she was with her male teachers in school. He asked her to give up her teaching role, so she could take care of the home.

Prior to the time, she had also been complaining of the backlog of work she had to do in school and how tiring it was to keep the home to Singh's standards. She refused to comply with Singh's instruction to quit her job. Gradually tension set in between the couple and depression beclouded Ewaoluwa's vision. She took to drinking at the local pub in the evenings after she finished marking her pupils' work or preparing her lessons. After a while, she got into the habit of getting drunk when Singh was at work in the evenings and at weekends. These habits took a toll on her personality and she became mindless and careless, which affected her work and manners in school. She often turned up in school with a hang over and an unappreciable level of anxiety.

By her second year in Smart Juniors School, she got suspended from school for being unruly in class. Sub consciously she had over reacted to a child that was extremely unruly and it led to domestic violence. When her teaching assistant tried to intervene, she was rude to him. At the end of the day, the child reported to her parents who took the matter up with the school. Whilst the matter was being investigated, she was suspended.

There had also been previous incidences when the other staffs weren't happy with her sudden personality change. After investigations, she was dismissed and taken to court. She was found to be unfit to continue teaching, so she was banned from teaching for a couple of years.

She was then forced to stay at home while Singh continued his managerial role in Convent Garden. Ewaoluwa became a nagging stay at home wife. She had more time to drink away her sorrows. She couldn't bear the thought of not having children and anytime she brought up the topic for discussion, it always ended in a heated verbal battle, accompanied by breaking of glasses and destruction of any item within reach. Singh couldn't put up with Ewaoluwa's constant nagging, violence and change of personality. He continued to spend more time at work than at home. Eventually he varnished from the home two years after they went to the registry.

She went shopping for grocery on a Thursday morning, and by the time she returned, Singh had packed all his things and left the flat for her. On her return, she was devastated and all frantic calls to get him to return proved abortive. She visited his work at Convent Garden, he had resigned and they withheld his where about. They feigned ignorance but told her that he had resigned that same day. She was left alone in the flat they had once shared. She was devastated, that wasn't the plan or her intention. Her breastplate of romance was missing and her heart was completely broken. Thursday, 22nd July 2004.

She spent the next year looking for a job. She wanted an office position so she picked up a job locally as a receptionist in Johnhill Broker. The salary was very low, the job was not so rewarding and the running expenses of the flat were quite high. Singh refused to contact her or communicate with her so she had to bear the financial burden of the flat alone. She was silently glad she was free from him. Although she loved him dearly, she wanted children and Singh couldn't have any nor was he willing to submit himself for corrective surgery.

After one year in their Kentish Town flat, she decided to look for another job, a cheaper accommodation and a fresh start without Singh. She assured herself that she would work hard, find a decent man, carry out her investigations on him, and if satisfied get married and have children.

She found another job as a waiter in The Duck in Wallington and moved to a rented room nearby. She found herself working in the bar section of the pub. She convinced herself that she would work hard like Singh and rise to a managerial position. Then she would be able to afford a flat of her own with time. Life was beginning to pick up once more for her.

However, the devil was really close to Ewaoluwa as she sought for another defensive armour. She met and fell in love with a Jamaican man she met in the Duck; Selwyn Matheson. He was into drugs and before long; Ewaoluwa was deep into drugs, sex and alcohol. The drugs took all she had, money, goals and even personality. Selwyn soon detected her addiction and couldn't maintain the supplies he gave her so he abandoned her. Although he was still a customer in The Duck, he warned her to stay clear of him or he would report her to the management. That was how she lost Selwyn; her second armour of defence.

At twenty nine years, Ewaoluwa was faced with poverty and homelessness. She also got a message that her mother, Temiloluwa was very ill. Her sisters, Ileriayo and Ileriolusesimi had employed carers to look after her in her Lagos residence whilst they continued with their family lives and businesses in Abuja. They also cared for their frail seventy nine years old father in Abuja so it was impossible to be in Lagos with their mother. Maintaining the carers posed its own challenges and soon it became obvious that Ewaoluwa's presence was needed at her mother's place, being the eldest child and daughter. Her seventy four years old mother requested that she came home to spend some time with her. She agreed and decided to go to Nigeria and help.

More so, she felt getting away from UK would deliver her from the lifestyle of drug and alcohol abuse she had fallen into. She thought she wouldn't be able to afford the drugs and there would be no one to supply, seeing that she never knew anyone who was into substance abuse. With no one to help her financially in UK, she soon turned herself in and voluntarily returned home. Ewaoluwa departed from UK with bitterness four years after she left the shores of Nigeria. Saturday 4th February 2006.

Chapter Three

BELT OF LOVE

The authorities organised her return home and she went back into teaching and looking after Temiloluwa who was very ill. The twenty nine years old taught at Achievers Infant School, Surulere. She gradually withdrew from drugs and alcohol because there was no ready supplier, besides she didn't want her mother to see her taking drugs. It would have been too much for her to take. The drug and alcohol withdrawal in Nigeria had a sober effect on her and the School she taught in attributed her mood and temperament were due to the change of environment and her mother's condition.

Temiloluwa eventually passed away and Ewaoluwa's seventy nine years old father was too fragile to attend the funeral. Temidire had also lost his second wife in Abuja about five years earlier and this had really affected him. Her sisters Ileriayo and Iriolusesimi came for the funeral with their families and left Lagos soon afterwards. It was after the funeral that Ewaoluwa began visiting Boogie Afrikana; a night club in Surulere.

After her mother's demise, Ewaoluwa plunged further into drugs and alcohol intake once more. She funded these habits from the income she got from her salary and her mother's estate. When these could not support her, she began to take out loans from her friends in Boogie Afrikana and soon she was deeply in debt. Her debtors insisted on recovering their loan from her salary and her share of her mother's estate. This put her in a distressed position, where she had to work very hard and take home very little pay. There was no longer anyone she could loan money from. Even her siblings deserted her.

Once again her destitute lifestyle took a toll on her personality; the school she taught in soon discovered it and fired her. Her condition grew worse and her teaching job which was meant to provide a sense of financial security for her as she resettled in Nigeria was no more. She not only lost the job she had also lost Temiloluwa; her main purpose in Nigeria.The news of her predicament soon got to her sisters in Abuja, but they couldn't really reach out to her. They were very busy professionals with families in Abuja and they were also looking after their aged father, Temidire. Through the help of her sisters' connections, Singh Ghandi was traced and contacted in UK. They informed him of

LOVE ON SEPARATE GROUNDS

Ewaoluwa's predicament and appealed to him to help. He promised to come down to Nigeria to see her.

However, he secretly planned to divorce her once she got better, so he could move on with his life and marry a homely domestic lady like his mother; Sadguna. He wanted someone who would be happy to stay at home and contented to live with him without having children. Singh arrived in Nigeria and was offered accommodation in Ewaoluwa's home. Over the years, her mother had built a duplex with two flats. Singh was accommodated on the lower flat because it was vacant at the time of his arrival. He had earlier heard about business potentials in Nigeria through the friend that encouraged him to come down and he had decided to explore the opportunities present on arrival. He pretended that he still loved Ewaoluwa so help can be readily available.

On seeing Ewaoluwa again, his heart sank. The attractiveness was still there though there were sad lines on her face. He saw that she really needed help and after making enquiries he was referred to Pansy's Chest Ibadan. He was determined not to get caught up in Ewaoluwa's affairs anymore so he was detached in all he did. On getting to Pansy's Chest, a young and handsome man walked over to them at the rehabilitation cluster. He introduced himself as Dr Oluiferiwa O'Figbayemi; the chief medical director's son. He had come to visit his father, Dr Praise O'Figbayemi. He was very chatty and flirty and Ewaoluwa subconsciously took to him. They met Dr Oluiferiwa on few more occasions during their visits to the rehabilitation chest and he was friendly on each visit. Ewaoluwa was also very friendly with him.

Singh soon noticed and became jealous and he began to harbour resentment towards Ewaoluwa. Eventually, he mentioned it to his good friend Hubert Knight; who encouraged him to come and make money in Nigeria. It was Hubert that contacted Singh when Ewaoluwa's sisters were investing his whereabouts. Hubert was a voluntary worker with different charity organisations in Nigeria and had good contacts in Pansy's Chest. He had recommended the place to Singh when he made enquiries about a drug rehabilitation centre and counselling unit, on his arrival in Nigeria.

Hubert advised Singh to confront the situation by making the doctor's son jealous. He was told to embrace her tightly as though he loved her and show some affection to her whenever Dr Oluiferiwa was around. Hubert also advised Singh to pay Ewaoluwa romantic and flirting comments; whispering sweet things into her ears. He was told to buy her flowers from the nearby shops on days they went to the rehabilitation sessions. They were both sure that Ewaoluwa would have the bouquet in her hands when they were inside the Chest. Singh believed that the suggested acts would caution the doctor.

Singh adhered to Hubert's suggestions and Ewaoluwa warmed up to him readily, without smelling the deception. Being back with Singh Ghandi had been her earnest cry from the day he varnished in UK two years earlier. He now responded to her in a manner that suggested that she could wrap him around her life once again, as she sought for comfort. She fantasized on how she could strap the relationship round her life, like a belt and bask in it while she recovered fully.

Moreover as her huge debt was being settled monthly from her mother's estate, there were no funds to cover her rehabilitation treatment. Through the consent of her father and sisters in Abuja, Singh agreed to move into Ewaoluwa's flat, which she had shared with her late mother. They rented out the flat Singh had occupied so they could afford her rehabilitation, treatment and maintenance cost. Singh drove her to Pansy's Chest twice a week to receive counselling and treatment. They met the counselling unit and missionaries who helped out there. These preached to them and encouraged them to embrace the new life characterised by forgiveness and passion for God. They told them about the God of restoration who makes all things and people new; despite their past. Singh and Ewaoluwa began to feel free with one another and embrace the freedom this new life provided.

LOVE ON SEPARATE GROUNDS

Soon the couple were able to talk about their marriage and discuss their personal life. They were encouraged in Pansy's Chest to leave their past behind and embrace their future together.

Singh was also encouraged to volunteer in the counselling unit on the days he brought Ewaoluwa into Pansy's Chest. He learnt about the christian faith in the Chest too. Ewaoluwa remembered the circumstances surrounding the collapse of their marriage but had decided to let go and embrace Singh. This was because he was the only family member that stood close, she had no choice. The implication of his presence meant that she had to be contented with the possibility of being barren. She had to hope that the future with Singh would be bright and he would really be the armour plate that would stand by her side and defend her.

Upon her recovery, Singh rediscovered her inner beauty once again and the love was rekindled in him. He now did the things he once did out of jealousy, out of love. Every night, he would express his love to her by instigating touches before bedtime. He cuddled her more often and soon they began to watch films and television programs together once more. With no job, Ewaoluwa soon became a couch potato; watching the television, listening to music and reading her favourite novels; Daniel Steel collections.

Now she felt better about Singh, as he made her feel good about herself once again. He treated her more like an equal and was more tender with his touches. She felt safe to be in his arms once more. He told her that he felt sorry that he had considered a divorce but now he was hopeful that their relationship would work out finer and better as a result of the counselling they received in Pansy's Chest. With regards to the issue of having children, they were advised to pray about the situation and either adopt a child, sponsor a child in an orphanage or consider the medical procedure, if they could afford it. The counsellors offered them a lot of hope.

The couple chose to settle down in Mercy Chapel, Surulere under the ministry of Reverend Olurantimi Omoba–Asejere who was the chaplain then. Ewaoluwa helped out in Sunday school. Once again Ewaoluwa began to send out her curriculum vitae in search of teaching roles and Singh signed a very good contract with Boogie Afrikana to be their manager. Life began to pick up for them in Nigeria as Singh was able to use his skills from the UK to improve on the management of the night club.

Ewaoluwa joined him on Friday nights at the night club to socialise with friends. They soon built a good social network support and through their contacts, Ewaoluwa began to work towards setting up her own nursery in her mother's house. The ground floor flat of her mother's house became vacant towards the middle of the year and Ewaoluwa opted to rent it herself. Singh was very helpful, as he saw it as a good investment opportunity. They planned to build a school gradually out of the nursery; starting from the rented flat below. Their long term goal was to buy their mother's house from the estate eventually; seeing it was in a prime location.

For about a year, Singh invested a good proportion of his savings into Ewaoluwa's nursery, so she called it Ewa Singh-Raj Nursery (ESRN). They also travelled to the United Kingdom twice that year for holidays. Theirs was a perfect union and it seems their marriage worked better in Nigeria. With the nursery in operation, Ewaoluwa had the children to keep her company. She was also able to get two nursery assistants to help out.

Ewaoluwa finished her work at the nursery one evening and went to her flat upstairs to relax as usual. She got a phone call that her attention was needed at the Boogie Afikana. She inquired if all was well and they told her that Singh had just been involved in an accident. He slumped in his office, after inspecting the stock in the cold room and was rushed to the hospital. Ewaoluwa screamed on hearing the news and suddenly hung up the phone. She was startled and confused.

LOVE ON SEPARATE GROUNDS

Where was she meant to go; hospital or the night club, and what was she meant to do? She could not remember. She panicked and kept missing her numbers as she tried to call the night club. About thirty minutes later, her door opened and one of the workers in the night club walked in. They offered to take her to the hospital where Singh was admitted. On getting there, Singh had passed away. He had suffered a heart attack and collapsed at his desk. Monday 15th January 2007.

Ewaoluwa was distraught and she burst into tears. Life had been so cruel; after all she had been through. Her marriage had just been restored and she was beginning to enjoy her marriage when Singh died unceremoniously. Ewaoluwa soon became dejected. She felt betrayed by life once again and lost interest in living. Mercy Chapel was at hand to offer their full support to Ewaoluwa.

However after a while, Ewaoluwa withdrew from the church and her activities under the pretence that she needed some time for herself. The pain was deep, that was double tragedy for her. In two years, she had lost her mother and husband and she was childless. Her nursery assistant ran the nursery while Ewaoluwa plunged into deep despair. Her sisters came for the funeral of Singh Ghandi with their families and left almost immediately afterwards. Boogie Afikana gave her a huge compensation sum to help her get back on her feet. The staff at Pansy's Chest also encouraged her to come for counselling when she felt the need to do so. The counsellors advised her to take her mind off the losses and do something positive with her life. She decided to continue with her education. She applied to go back to the university for her masters programme the following year. It was a three year part time course. There she met three friends who would later become her life long friends. They were Tiana Noire Ileanuoluwakishu, Habiba Mohammed and Chioma Etti, all undergraduates. Thursday 4th September 2008.

During her academic program, she was very discreet about her visits to Pansy's Chest and worked in her nursery on part time basis. She silently grieved so much from Singh's death that all dating attempts she made in school failed. In 2011 when her friends went to do their youth service, Ewaoluwa continued running ESGN with her staff. This kept her mind from thinking about Singh Ghandi; the protective armour that she had lost. Shortly after their service year, one of her friends, Tiana left for UK to meet her fiancé and they gathered round to hold a send forth for her.

Chapter Four

SHIELD OF LOVE

Whenever she was around in Pansy's Chest, she saw the chief medical director; Dr Praise O'Figbayemi who was resident there. He and his wife Oluwadamisi had five children, all grown up, married and working in different parts of the country. The first was a consultant doctor in Lagos University Teaching Hospital but he later got into politics. The second was an Engineer in Port Harcourt, the third was a lawyer in Abia State, the fourth was an accountant in Kano State and the fifth was a missionary in Kogi State. They all graduated in their early twenties with first class. Ewaoluwa regularly ran into the eldest child, Dr Oluiferiwa in the Chest too.

On her thirty fifth birthday in 2012, Ewaoluwa had a thanksgiving at Mercy Chapel, and invited few friends to lunch. The house was filled with guests including Reverend Olurantimi who had retired a month before her event. Also present were the current chaplain; Reverend Iyanuloluwa and his wife Lady Davina Igbagbo-Durotimi. They prayed for her and left, soon afterwards Dr Oluiferiwa arrived. He brought a bouquet of flowers and a gift for her. At the end of the lunch, Dr Oluiferiwa thanked her and left.

After all the guests had left in the evening, she opened the gift Dr Oluiferiwa gave her. In it were lingerie and a jewellery set containing a pair of gold earrings and choker chain with matching bracelets. He later called her in the night to express his desire to have a relationship with her. She thanked him for the gift and said that his request to date her had come to her as a surprise and the most beautiful birthday gift. Ewaoluwa thought having a relationship and getting married to Dr Oluiferiwa may provide the much needed shield.

The following day, after the nursery closed for the day, a black Model 3 electric car, Lexus new IS 300h drove into her compound. It was Dr Oluiferiwa, she was stunned. She didn't know the doctor was that rich. He took her to the Happy Hour Restaurant, Obalende for dinner and they had some jacket potatoes and stewed pork with peas, broccoli, sprouts, and butternut squash. They also had a glass of red wine each with their dinner. As they ate, Dr Oluiferiwa asked her about her background and she told him about her childhood and marriage to Singh Ghandi. He already knew about her drug challenges from the first day he met them at Pansy's Chest when she came for a rehabilitation session with Singh Ghandi.

He said he was sorry she had lost her very caring husband. He thought they were really close and said he felt extremely jealous anytime they came round to the Chest. He then proceeded to tell her about his childhood. He said that he was the first of his parents' five children and was a consultant doctor in Lagos University Teaching Hospital. In recent years he has been involved in politics and aspires to be a minister of health someday. While he loved swimming and playing lawn tennis, Ewaoluwa said she loved reading novels and watching films. As they talked, the chemistry between the two increased which pleased Ewaoluwa.

Once again, she had hoped for a shield that would screen her from the harshness of loneliness and also guard her from her drug addictions. She knew she had what it took to excel but she was also aware of her vulnerability at that stage of her life. She also knew that she needed support so she could regain her financial strength. The question she then had to ask herself was if Dr Oluiferiwa could provide the bulwark of love to help her pull through. She expressed her fears and he responded in the affirmative and told her to give him a chance to try.

LOVE ON SEPARATE GROUNDS

After dinner, he ordered a bottle of cognac to toast to their first outing. Next a waiter brought a large birthday cake and got few other waiters to sing a birthday song to Ewaoluwa. She was so overwhelmed and burst into tears. It was just what she needed after Singh Ghandi died. Hopefully, she could have a child or two with Dr Oluiferiwa, if the relationship ended up in marriage. The relationship would shield her from the unpleasant experience of drug addiction and the children would serve as a lubricant to protect against the cruelty meted out to barren women in Nigeria.

After dinner, they drove to Dr Oluiferiwa's home in Ikoyi where they met two ladies. Fifteen year old Mobolade and thirteen year old Olufayokunmi were introduced as his daughters from a previous relationship. The teenagers greeted her nicely and left the room. He took her round the house. His home was nicely decorated with flowers and his children's room had posters of celebrities on the walls. He attributed the beautiful deco to his first wife's love for interior decoration. He told her that he also loved antiques, especially the ones from Nigeria.

Afterwards, they both sat down to watch a movie. She had told him that she didn't believe in sex before marriage, so he took her home afterwards. With each passing second, he was proving to be more of a bulwark of love and support; the key things she was looking for in a relationship. Singh

LOVE ON SEPARATE GROUNDS

Ghandi had also been a bulwark of love to her in the first and last few months of their marriage.

They had dinner together every night for the rest of the week and each time, they ended up in Dr Oluiferiwa's Ikoyi residence. They courted for about six months during which Ewaoluwa was formerly introduced as his fiancé. She met his friends, parents and other four siblings. They all loved Ewaoluwa because she was a very intelligent and smart lady. She was also an intellectual with proven academic records; just what the O'Figbayemi family needed to complement them.

In the course of their engagement, he assisted her in re branding ESGN to incorporate both nursery and primary schools. Ewa Singh-Raj Nursery (ESRN) then became Ewa Singh-Raj Schools (ESRS) with classes running up to year three. Although she was a very bold fighter, with masculine personality, she had been marred by life's experiences but being under the mentorship of Lady Davina, the chaplain's wife, her character was reformed and she learnt to be very humble to her fiance.

In her seventh month of dating Dr Oluiferiwa and getting used to the family, she began to pressurise him into marriage. When all her attempts failed, she eventually conceded to sex before marriage, using it as a tool to motivate him to get married. Prior to that he was contented with abstinence. Lady Davina wasn't aware of the new development so she continued to encourage her in the path of holiness. Dr Oluiferiwa was a non practising christian so Ewaoluwa got away with quite a number of ungodly activities.

Ewaoluwa finally moved in with Dr Oluiferiwa and his daughters. Her life was once again coming together as she found love in his arms. His attitude changed soon afterwards. He started spending a lot of time in his private clinic and when he was home, he was always in his study. Ewaoluwa was left to care for his two daughters; Mobolade and Olufayokunmi. The only comfort she had was the fact that the family safe guarded her from her destructive habits and no one appeared to contend with her role by Dr Oluiferiwa's side. She was also sure of the likelihood of her having children with Dr Oluiferiwa.

However, in the eleventh month of their relationship, Ewaoluwa returned from ESGS to see a lady waiting for her in Dr Oluiferiwa's Ikoyi residence. Ewaoluwa went ahead to introduce herself proudly as Dr Oluiferiwa's fiancée and the lady introduced herself as Ilemobola, the mother of Mobolade and Olufayokunmi. She thanked Ewaoluwa for looking after the children in her absence. Ewaoluwa was shocked! It appeared Ilemobola hadn't heard what she had said. She had told her that she was Dr Oluiferiwa's fiancée.

LOVE ON SEPARATE GROUNDS

What did Ilemobola mean by thanking her for looking after the children in her absense'?

Ilemobola told her that she was sorry the guest room wasn't well ventilated but now she's back, she would try and organise a better ventilation system for the room. She told Ewaoluwa that she could not afford to look after the children when she was studying in the US so she sent them to live with their father in Nigeria, whilst she completed her studies. Now her studies were over and she was back for her family. Ewaoluwa panicked and became confused. What? She thought to herself. Dr Oluiferiwa had told her that the children were products of a relationship that failed. He told her that the mother didn't want to take responsibility for the children so he decided to have full custody. She believed him because the children confirmed the story that their mother didn't want them and that was what gave her the courage to fully embrace them. As she was trying to compose herself, Mobolade and Olufayokunmi both came out and thanked Ewaoluwa for her kindness. They gave her a large bouquet of flowers each. She burst into tears.

'Where did that leave her', she thought to herself? 'No she was going to fight. She could not let go easily, at least Ilemobola wasn't married to Oluiferiwa, or was she'? She then remembered Dr Praise O'Figbayemi saying that all his children were married. 'What happened to her hearing? What did she just do'? She had promised herself since the time Singh Ghandi varmished that she would do a thorough investigation on the next man that wanted to marry her. Once again, in desperation, she had thrown caution into the wind.

'Did it mean that they approved of his adulterous living and played on her emotions? Why didn't anyone in the O'Figbayemi family caution them'? Not even their friends had confronted her while they went out together. They watched him as he helped her in rebranding ESGS and they saw all she did to help him raise his political profile. 'So that was it? That was the trade in? That was the secret behind the success of the so called prestigious family'?

Ewaoluwa went out of the living room angrily and made way for the bedroom which she shared with Oluiferiwa. On getting there, she discovered that he had moved her things to the guest room and Ilemobola's suit cases were in the bedroom instead. This new protective coating she had guarded her life with was proving to be a harsh abrasive after all; an abrasive that would erode her of love and happiness. She began to scream at him in disgust. She asked him why he lied to her about Ilemobola. He denied lying. He said that she had left them for her studies and Ewaoluwa gave him a slap.

He got enraged, locked the door to the bedroom and gave her a thorough beating. Then he sent her out of the house and threw her things on the street. In a twinkle of an eye, her whole fantasy about Dr Oluiferiwa and his family providing a shield of love for her gave way. It was too late, she had lost control in a split second and the doctor wasn't going to take it. She came back inside the house and tried to beg him to reconsider but it was too late. He told her that the slap was the seal that ended the relationship. He called a taxi, put her things in it, pushed her into it and paid the driver to take her back to the Surulere flat she had shared with her late mother.

Ewaoluwa appealed to the taxi to help her drop her things at the reception of ESGS. She had to sleep in one of the rooms that she used as an office on the ground floor because she was very sore from the beating that she received. She had headaches, body pains and a cut below her eye. She was in pain and alone throughout the night. By the next morning when her staff came to open the nursery, she had passed out. They found her drenched in blood. Ewaoluwa, the headteacher was found on the floor of her office all beaten up. She was given first aid and rushed to the hospital. The staff reported the matter to the police who came and searched the entire building for proof of burglary. They found no trace. By the evening, she was fine but quiet. She later told the police what happened and it was recorded as domestic violence. Ewaoluwa said that she wasn't going to press for charges and the police left.

LOVE ON SEPARATE GROUNDS

She ordered her staff to move out all the things in the library on the upper floor and transfer them to the children's activity area downstairs. The room would then be converted to a live in flat for her, since it was en-suite and had an open kitchenette. That was how she returned to her mother's home.

All her attempt at reconciling with Dr Oluiferiwa failed. That was the end of the beautiful relationship with him. He had used her to look after his children and fill the gap created by Ilemobola. He had presented her to everyone as his fiancé and had kept her away from other suitors. Through her influence, she had also helped him build his political career. He had used her for some other political events. Now she was embittered; not only had she lost a lover, another year had been stolen from her.

She pulled herself together as she tried to date four other men in the next one year, from their circle of influence but the relationships all fizzled out. These were men who had indicated their interest in her when she was still in the relationship with Dr Oluiferiwa. Whenever she got close, they hinted her that they didn't need her slap and drifted away. She felt as though he knew her desperation for a man and programmed the four men she dated into her life to disappoint her. After the last man ditched her on account of not desiring 'an unwanted slap', she vowed that she was going to revenge.

LOVE ON SEPARATE GROUNDS

The doctor was done with having a relationship with her, yet he stalked her. He wasn't going to have her and he wasn't going to let another man take her. She would take out her revenge on Dr Oluiferiwa, his children and their mother. She would try her best to gather enough political strength to carry out her revenge. She would leave the family dejected and destitute; from Dr Oluiferiwa's father to his siblings, children and their mother, Ilemobola. All she wanted was love. All she wanted was her own children. All she wanted was her own family. All she got was betrayal and hurt. Now she was going to get the power to revenge at all cost. At last, what came into her life to shield her initially had failed. She must seek for a protective armour, but this time it would be to carry out a dastardly act; to revenge on the wrong done to her.

Chapter Five

SWORD OF LOVE

In the next couple of months she secretly planned how she was going to carry out her vengeance while her staff at ESGS thought that she had gotten over the disappointment of the broken courtship with Dr Oluiferiwa. She soon ran into her old friends that took drugs with her and got her supplies from them at Boogie Afrikana. She was able to maintain the lifestyle with the money she got from her nursery and her late mother's estate. Her plan was to implicate Dr Praise O'Figbayemi and his son in drug trafficking. She believed that this would put them out of work and behind bars for a couple of years. She would go through Pansy's Chest and pretend she needed help.

The parents of ESGS pupils soon noticed that she wasn't her usual self. Unlike the previous time in UK when she lost her teaching role due to unruly behaviour, she was now more discreet with her activities. She was found out when a parent walked into her in Boogie Afrikana and caught her in the act. The parent felt it was unethical for a school proprietor to be caught in such an act and decided to make a fuss about it. The parent raised a campaign against her and other parents who shared similar views soon placed a demand for a board of trustees to take over the running of ESGS. The trustees passed a referendum and told her that they couldn't entrust the whole management of the school to her again. She would have to work with them.

By then she had seven classes of fifteen children each, seven teachers, four teaching assistants and an administrator. In the last one year, she had made significant progress with ESGS while she dated the affluent Dr Oluiferiwa. Just when she felt she had everything under control, Ilemobola turned up and the O'Figbayemis' skeleton fell out of the cupboard. To her, it was more like a collaboration to deceive than the doctor was a flirt. They all knew what he was doing to her but had kept quiet. This was one of the strong reasons that fuelled her desire for a chronic revenge. After painstakingly running ESGS for eight years, this was all she got; disgrace. Ewaoluwa now sought for a sword to use to destroy the doctor and his family.

However, on a particular day as she came out of the nightclub, looking very high on drugs, she ran into Hubert, Singh's friend. He approached her to greet her but she ignored him and pretended that she didn't know him. He felt embarrassed but left her. He had been at Singh's funeral in 2007 but had lost touch. He later heard that she was engaged to Doctor Praise O'Figbayemi's eldest son. Later in the evening, Hubert told his wife Kathy about how poorly Ewaoluwa had looked when he bumped into her at Boogie Afrikana. They both decided to contact her other friend Chioma who was a banker at Marine Bank Victoria Island. Chioma in turn notified Habiba. The three friends hadn't heard from Tiana since she left for UK in 2012 so they decided to go look for Ewaoluwa and help her without Tiana.

Chioma and Habiba went and paid Ewaoluwa a visit in her school and on seeing them, she burst into tears. She narrated her misery with Dr Oluiferiwa. Habiba informed her that she heard that she had been dealing in drugs. She wanted her to explain why she did it and the reason she felt that was the way out. Up until then, Ewaoluwa was silent on her previous life with Singh Ghandi. She was then forced to tell her friends about her first marriage and late husband and the circumstances that led her into substance abuse.

In addition, Ewaoluwa told them that it was Selwyn Matheson that introduced her to it when he sensed she was desperate for a partner in UK. She said she was aware of the implication and was trying to get out. She told them that she periodically went to Pansy's Chest for counselling and help. She also confided in them that it was her dark secret and begged them to keep Tiana out of it. They promised to keep quiet and help her. They also informed her that Hubert had promised to help in his own little way.

Habiba was a business woman who owned a restaurant franchise. She was responsible for ensuring Ewaoluwa freed herself from her destructive lifestyle and ate wholesome meals regularly. Ewaoluwa frowned at their sudden intrusion initially but as she couldn't justify or explain away the trauma she felt, she gave in and allowed her friends to access her life. As she went for her therapy sessions in Pansy's Chest, she began to strategise on how to implicate Dr Praise O'Figbayemi and his son Dr Oluiferiwa. She needed a sword that would pierce their heart and cause total devastation for the pains they had cost her.

Meanwhile, Chioma and Habiba held a meeting with the trustees of ESGS. They negotiated with them to repossess the rest of the upper flat of ESGS building. They planned to convert it back to a residential flat where Ewaoluwa could live comfortably. Up until then, she had occupied only a room on the upper floor. It had been used solely as a play and activity area for ESGS children. Hubert then used his influence as a voluntary worker with various charities in Nigeria to help revive the image of ESGS. Ewaoluwa slowly began to make progress again. Mercy Chapel wasn't aware that she became despondent after her separation from Dr Oluiferiwa, though they later heard the rumour that she had moved in with him during her engagement. On hearing her recovery story, Lady Davina promised to keep an extra eye on her. Ewaoluwa later found out that the chaplain's three children, Faith, Hope and Love had attended Achievers Infant School, where she first taught on her return to Nigeria. She was thankful they never met because she was fired and that would have been too embarrassing for her. The children were now in Achievers' High School.

Despite the love she received from Mercy Chapel, Ewaoluwa adamantly sought for a sword to wreck havoc on the O'Figbayemi family but so far all she found were swords of love. The fact that she had lost a great deal in terms of integrity, reputation, time, and ego made her to ignore all the kind gestures. She knew that it was only by a stroke of luck that she didn't lose the ownership of ESGS. She went on to make friends with very popular people as she continued to look for ways to wage war on the O'Figbayemi family.

One of the eminent people she met on her return to her Surulere flat was Chief Alfred Costcutter, a Port Harcourt indigene, who was a heavy dealer in drugs. She became close to him and when she felt he was falling in love, she confided in him that she wanted to implicate Dr Praise O'Figbayemi and his son. He suggested that she introduced a treasure hunt in Pansy's Chest. She asked him what he meant. He explained that it involved planting small pouches filled with drugs in and around the doctor's office and accommodation anytime she went for her theraphy sessions. The pouches would have his signature engraved on them.

After dropping them, they would arrange for a grapevine to notify the patients coming for the drug rehabilitation sessions that he was a hypocrite and a notorious dealer in drugs. He promised to help her spread the rumour in Ibadan and also promised to supply her with tiny pouches of drugs in exchange for sex. She got desperate and agreed as she didn't have money to pay up. She felt the doctors deserved it and she wanted the entire family which they placed so much pride in to crumble.

The next time Ewaoluwa went into Pansy's Chest, she was accompanied by Alfred and his gang. They all pretended that they were strangers to one another. They were elegantly dressed and went on the tour round Pansy's Chest; only Ewaoluwa went for her usual therapy sessions. They dropped the tiny drug pouches in the most concealed yet easily assessable places. For the next couple of weeks, Alfred sent different groups of people to the Chest and these went on the daily tours. They dropped a significant number of the pouches engraved with the doctor's signature in the entire Chest. Soon it was observed that there was large turn out of people in the recreation cluster of Pansy's Chest. They seem to be all excited and eager to go on tour round the Chest. While the doctor and his team ran a drug rehabilitation program at the therapy cluster, there was a cartel of people that secretly dropped pouches of drugs and another group that happily picked them up for free from where they were hidden. They all left Pansy's Chest excited.

Though it was a drug prohibited site, visitors within the Chest found small pouches of drugs hidden within it. The grapevine quickly spread throughout the country that while the management of Pansy's Chest prohibited the use of illegal drugs on site and the medical team campaigned against its use, the chief medical director; Doctor Praise O'Figbayemi secretly distributed it on site. They claimed that he did it to gain favour in the sight of the rich and powerful so that they could help his son in politics. They also claimed that he did it so as to command more revenue within the Chest. It was rumoured that the revenue generated from the tours alone were now more than the total generated by the other facilities within the Chest.

This caused a lot of embarrassment for the management and a panel was set up to conduct an enquiry. Dr Praise O'Figbayemi and his son were probed, since Dr Oluiferiwa was a frequent visitor to the Chest. During his probation, Dr Praise O'Figbayemi was temporarily relieved of his duties but allowed to remain in the medical team's cluster. His son was also invited for periodic interrogations. This affected Doctor Praise O'Figbayemi's morale and also humiliated his family.

A thorough investigation was conducted and he was later re-instated as the chief medical director of Pansy's Chest. The findings were linked to mischievous and deviant acts carried out by vindictive members of the public whom they had opened their doors to. It was never traced to Ewaoluwa. The management tendered a public apology to users and visitors of the site. They acknowledged that while the site was once a notorious ground for drug addicts, the present management had taken an oath to keep drugs off the site. They purported that it was probably someone from the past who wanted to revive the era of substance abuse on the site.

The authorities moved swiftly to action and mounted stiffer security measures on site. They also installed CCTV cameras and made the users on site aware of the security measures they took in ensuring a safer environment for those that came for the drug rehabilitation exercise. The awareness of the safety measures made Alfred and his gang desist from dropping pouches on the site. Although Ewaoluwa paid dearly with her body night after night, she was satisfied that she had ridiculed the O'Figbayemi family temporarily. The result of her actions had introduced shame and lots of pain within the prestigious family. When Dr Praise O'Figbayemi couldn't take it any more, he developed health challenges. He resumed back in office quite frail and humiliated.

Neither Chioma nor Habiba suspected the mischief; all they knew was that Ewaoluwa went to Pansy's Chest frequently for counselling sessions. She had carried out her mischief in Pansy's Chest through the help of her close buddy, Alfred. Although Alfred dealt in drugs, he did it in a manner that was very discreet; been a highly influential public figure. He wasn't married but rumour had it that he had strings of ladies who had children for him. He had his way with women as he was always seen rescuing vulnerable women and Ewaoluwa was his latest victim.

In the next twelve months, Chioma and Habiba provided all the help Ewaoluwa needed to maintain the integrity of ESGS and stay off drugs. Despite their tight schedule, they frequently visited Ewaoluwa to monitor her progress so she had the trustees to report to on the management of the ESGS and her friends to report to on the management of her life.

Eventually Tiana called from UK to say that she fell out with her fiancé and was due to come back to Nigeria in two years time. Her three friends Ewaoluwa, Chioma and Habiba had been sorry that the fiancé she met through the online dating had disappointed her in UK. Although they were silent on Ewaoluwa's inglorious past with drugs, they informed her of the progress of ESGS and she was pleased. Tiana was also taking short courses in child health care and had considered teaching as an alternative, if she didn't find any job in the healthcare sector on her arrival in Nigeria.

The year 2017 was a memorable year for the four friends. Firstly, Tiana came back from UK with her friends on a mission on Tuesday 18th April 2017. Ewaoluwa, Chioma and Habiba received them and helped them get around. Later that year, Chioma finally got everything that she needed to study for her masters program in UK and she departed on Friday 1st September 2017. Habiba also met her fiancé, Khatumu Mansir at a business function earlier in the year and they got married on Saturday 7th October 2017. Both Ewaoluwa and Tiana were the bride's maids. Tiana also became pregnant, got married at Ikoyi registry on Saturday 16th December 2017 and left for UK with her fiancé two weeks later. Ewaoluwa also received the best support she could get from her friends and bounced back strongly to the amazement of everyone, including the trustees of ESGS. It was indeed a year of total restoration and turn around for her.

LOVE ON SEPARATE GROUNDS

Tiana got back to Sanderstead on Saturday 30th December 2017 and both Ewaoluwa and Tiana kept in touch afterwards.

Ewaoluwa had been very instrumental to Tiana's teaching career in Nigeria and had promised to link her up with a nice partner. After the birth of Tiana's twin babies on 12th February 2018, she was inspired to set up a nursery, so she could work round her children. While considering it, she met a couple with similar interest, who were looking for business partners. The Littlewoods had secured a public building and hoped to start the new nursery at the start of spring.

Although they had registered few children, they were yet to recruit the staff. They offered Tiana the opportunity to join them because of her educational background in children's healthcare. They knew they needed extra hands once the school started and confided in Tiana that they could only afford temporary staff initially for economic reasons. Tiana welcomed the partnering role because it provided swift acceleration for her. It would save her the time and energy she would have spent in conducting business research and setting up the business. It was also a cheaper and more effective way of realising her dreams faster. She didn't have the level of experience and expertise needed to run a nursery. Her own concept was to start with the basic children's day care and gradually work her way up. The journey ahead may be far and laborious unless she accepted the offer. She saw the Littlewoods as God sent.

However, Tiana didn't want to be the only black lady amongst the whites, so she contacted Ewaoluwa and told her of the opportunity available in Sanderstead Tiny Feet. Ewaoluwa thanked Tiana for the opportunity and also used the occasion to tell her of her previous life with Singh Ghandi; emphasizing on her teaching experience in UK and Nigeria. Tiana was shocked that she had kept a major part of her adult life a secret for so long. None of her friends had detected it in all the years. They never questioned the name of the school or its formation. Ewaoluwa had told them that Singh Ghandi was one of the financial sponsors of ESGS and they had assumed it was a UK company that invested in the school. The disclosure was shocking but Tiana welcomed it because it meant that if Ewaoluwa accepted the offer, it would be easier to bring her on board than an outsider. It meant she wasn't naïve to the UK system like Tiana had been. It also meant that she had good teaching exposure and experience in UK which Tiana could glean from.

Tiana ran the idea by her husband Jayden and he seemed okay with it. She then recommended Ewaoluwa to her partners; the Littlewoods. She told them of her experience both as a teacher in UK and a head teacher in Nigeria. After much deliberation, it was agreed that they would harness Ewaoluwa's experience and use the model to develop Sanderstead Tiny Feet's holiday club. They planned to run teachers' exchange programs which they believe would also help Ewaoluwa in Nigeria and UK.

The Littlewoods then thought about applying for government funding. They had the idea of incorporating sustainability 'Around The Globe' in the teachers' exchange program. This would run during the summer holidays. They approached the London borough of Croydon and the education board with the initiative. A series of consultations were held and it was agreed that the teachers from the British infant and junior schools liase with the Littlewoods to produce the framework for the programme. The program was later developed to accommodate few teachers from within and outside Europe. These would participate and observe during the holidays. An area of international interest would be inculcating the awareness of sustainability and global warming in children as young as five. A planning committee was set up and they had grants from the government to help them implement the programme. They were granted the permission to carry out their pilot scheme in the summer of that year. 24th April 2018

Chapter Six

ACTS OF LOVE

She hung up the phone after speaking with her father, Temidire Tolulope who resided in Abuja. Temidire had been pivotal in her choice of career when she couldn't make up her mind on what to do. Now she was so full of thanks to him. He called her 'teacher' since childhood because he learnt a lot about life through his children; Ewaoluwa was the eldest. She packed her suitcases and left for the airport. She was assisted by the ESGS administrator and another seasoned teacher whom she put in charge to hold forth till she returned. Her staff had gathered to have a farewell dinner for Ewaoluwa as she proceeded to the UK on the teachers' exchange program. Saturday, 26th May 2018.

Tiana had invited her to the UK to participate in the program over the summer because she had been sold out to rendering random acts of love since she got married in 2017. Tiana had achieved more than she could have imagined and knew it was due to the random acts of love she had received since birth. As another act of love, she offered Ewaoluwa the opportunity to live in the Freeman cottage while she attended the program. The Freeman family had a Spanish house keeper and an Irish nanny, so Ewaoluwa didn't think she would have much challenges with the family. Tiana had also promised to stand beside her in selecting a responsible future partner before she returned to Nigeria.

The forty one year old Ewaoluwa arrived at Gatwick airport the following morning and made her way to Sanderstead. On arrival at the cottage, she met Tiana walking the dogs; a chore she mentioned to Ewaoluwa that she enjoyed doing from time to time. The two friends were thrilled to see each other and they had a lot to talk about from their days in the university till their lives afterwards.

Firstly, Tiana introduced Ewaoluwa to her family and showed her the guest room on the ground floor. After she had freshened up, the two friends had breakfast together. It was a typical English breakfast consisting of bread, baked beans, mushrooms, onions, bacon, sausages and eggs. Tiana's three months old twins; Chrysan and Marie had baby cereals. Ewaoluwa found the breakfast rich and moorish and she thanked Grandma Rose for preparing it. She also thanked the Freeman family for inviting her to stay.

LOVE ON SEPARATE GROUNDS

After breakfast, the twin's babbles were heard in their rooms while Alannah, their Irish nanny kept an eye on them. She had taken over from Rita a month earlier to allow Rita enough time to help Tiana and the Littlewoods in setting up Sanderstead Tiny Feet. Like Rita, Alannah was so adorable and chatty that Tiana thought of absorbing her in the nursery too. Alannah was an introvert, so the demand to take the babies out reduced. She took them to the library and Sanderstead Activity Group on Saturdays while they attended the crèche in Sanderstead Tiny Feet on weekdays.

Later on, Grandma Rose went to the breakfast section in the kitchen to listen to the radio while Grandpa George played the piano in the living room. Jayden had gone to work next door before Ewaoluwa's arrival. Tiana took her round the home and garden, and they chatted as they walked in the garden. Ewaoluwa asked Tiana about Chioma and she said that she hadn't heard from Habiba nor Chioma since she arrived in Sanderstead. Habiba had been silent since her wedding to Safiyanu Mansir in Nigeria and Chioma had been silent since she went to Birmingham for her masters.

Being a very busy person, Tiana didn't have much time to follow up on her friends; she was busy being a mother to her three months old twins as well as overseeing the Freeman Home and Garden. She also worked with the Littlewoods in setting up Sanderstead Tiny Feet which had opened its doors on Monday 2nd April 2018. While they walked in the garden, Ewaoluwa noticed that there were a number of animals there to her amazement. She had seen fruit, crop, vegetable and arid farms in Nigeria but animal farms were places she had only read about in books. She got envious of Tiana; her friend seemed to be doing very well for herself. They spent the whole morning in the garden. Jayden came home for lunch and was happy to see Ewaoluwa once again. The last time he saw her was when she came for their farewell gathering in Nigeria. Grandma Rose had prepared some fresh salad, steak and rice.

After lunch, Tiana took Ewaoluwa to Sandersted Tiny Feet popularly referred to as STF. It was a very nice and child friendly environment, fully equipped with children's play equipments and open ground for the children to play. The Littlewoods had made provision for twenty children but they had sixteen children; including four babies, registered and enrolled. Being a Saturday, no child was there.

On getting back home, they had jacket potatoes and stewed pork with peas, broccoli, sprouts, and butternut squash for dinner. Once again Ewaoluwa thanked Grandma Rose for preparing the meals and inviting her to partake of them. After getting the children in bed, Tiana handed Ewaoluwa a Daniel Steel collection to read in bed, she remembered Ewaoluwa loved the novels. Ewaoluwa lay in her bed and admired the lilac painted walls with wooden skirting and cornice painted in mint. She then opted to watch a movie on the television and reserved the novels for some other day.

The Freeman home had Irish meals on Sundays because Grandma Rose was originally Irish. The following Sunday, she prepared welsh rarebit for breakfast. Ewaoluwa loved the melted cheese on buttered toast with tomatoes, peas and sausages. Afterwards Tiana and Ewaoluwa went with the twins to the local church by bus whilst Jayden took his parents to church in the car. She planned to return to the children's church once Ewaoluwa settled in and they had enough hands in the nursery.

For lunch, the family had roast potatoes and roast beef in Yorkshire pudding and vegetables. They also had some fruits afterwards. After lunch, the five adults settled to a board game and watched Coronation Street together. Alannah was off duty on Sunday so while Tiana helped Grandma Rose with the dinner which was welsh lamb cawl, Ewaoluwa sat and watched Jayden play with the twins. Though she didn't fancy the dinner which consist of potatoes, carrots, leeks, lamb, parsnip, swede and crusty bread, she thanked Grandma Rose and Tiana for preparing them.

LOVE ON SEPARATE GROUNDS

After dinner, as was the custom, the family sat down to listen to Grandpa George play hymns of praise to God and Grandma Rose said the evening prayer, before the family retreated to their quiet corner; each to his own activity. In her room, Ewaoluwa felt really stuffed up, this was quite different to the Nigerian meals she was used to. She smiled as she remembered the standard Sunday meals she had back in Nigeria. She had beans pudding and pap or custard for breakfast, pounded yam and melon soup with stewed beef for lunch and chicken fried rice with sweet and sour pork for dinner. She was grateful for the starch reduction meals in the Freeman home in UK and she hoped to lose her belly fat.

The next day was a bank holiday and the whole family decided to mark it quietly, as Ewaoluwa settled into the Freeman household. On Tuesday 29th May 2018, Alannah got the twins ready for the crèche while Tiana took Ewaoluwa to register with the doctor and other relevant agencies. They proceeded to Sandersted Tiny Feet which (STF) was off Sanderstead High Street. On getting to the school, Tiana introduced Ewaoluwa to Alexia and Bryce who after greeting her, asked her to tell them about her experience.

Ewaoluwa told them that prior to her founding ESGS in 2006, she had experienced an undulating progress in her teaching profession. She had her masters degree in education from the university in 2011 and her first degree in the same course and same university in 2000. In between, she had been a teacher at Achievers Infant School, Surulere in 2006, Smart Juniors School Kentish Town from 2002 – 2004 and Bright Minds Montessory Private School Abuja in 2001, where she did her National Youth Service programme.

Bryce then went ahead to brief Ewaoluwa about himself and Alexia. Bryce Littlewoood said that he had been Jayden's childhood friend and both attended the same local church. He never left Sanderstead but stayed on to become a seasoned and experienced infant and junior school teacher. He and his wife Alexia were also neighbours to Rita, who lived on the same street with the Freeman family. They had rented the school property and registered STF with the educational board. He further went on to say that on hearing that Tiana wanted to set up a crèche, they had invited her to partner with them. They coveted her healthcare skills as well as her management and administrative skills. She was brought on board to assist with the administration of the new school as well as teach and work as a first aid worker. Through her influence, the Freeman Garden was contracted to supply the dairy needs of STF. This was another economical option for the Littlewoods.

Alexia welcomed Ewaoluwa and told her that she would be allowed to observe STF for two weeks, before being allowed to work in the capacity of a volunteer staff. She would then be given a probation period of another two weeks, and upon satisfactory performance, she would be enrolled for the two months teachers' exchange programme under the school's covering.

It was then time for the classes to begin their sessions. Alannah and Rita were put in charge of the crèche, and Tiana taught the reception class how to read the alphabets. The younger children sat down as they were entertained to songs and games by Bryce. After the first hour, Alexia divided the class and supervised the boys in playing with the computer, while Bryce and the girls played with soft toys and Tiana continued with the reception class. In the next hour, the class was mixed again and re grouped. Some children chose to read story books and Tiana read to them while others preferred to draw and paint with Bryce leading the class.

Ewaoluwa joined Alannah and Rita in serving dinner. The older children had chicken or fish nuggets with green vegetables while the babies were given food provided by their parents. Then it was time for the out door activities. Bryce engaged some children in sand craft and Alexia engaged others in water craft. Tiana ensured the health and safety rules were adhered to. Ewaoluwa also assisted with clearing up.

After their break, the girls played with the computer, the boys were given soft toys to play with. On completion of their activities, Bryce played music and took some older children in dancing class while Alexia took the others in singing and acting. When it was time to leave, Tiana and Ewaoluwa walked back home with Alannah, who pushed the twin buggy. On the way, Ewaoluwa was impressed by the numerous high street shops and Tiana promised to bring her window shopping over the weekend.

While Tiana helped Grandma Rose with lunch, Ewaoluwa was encouraged to watch the news. She had heard so much about the Queen and the royal family. Now she had a chance to hear more about them from the television as she watched the documentary on them. She hoped to visit Windsor Castle before departing from UK at the end of the exchange program. Unlike Tiana, she was very inquisitive and eager to explore. Tiana also promised to take her on a tour to places of interest.

While Ewaoluwa was relaxing with Tiana in the garden in the evening, a tall, dark and handsome Indian man walked into the garden. He nodded to Tiana before heading to the south garden. Tiana introduced him as Singh Raj, the garden manager. Ewaoluwa's heart skipped and she plunged into a prolonged silence. Memories of Singh Ghandi flushed through her mind once again. Like Singh Ghandi, Ewaoluwa found Singh so attractive that her heart longed for him. It appeared she had an affinity for Indian men.

LOVE ON SEPARATE GROUNDS

She soon confessed to Tiana that she had developed a crush on Singh. Tiana smiled encouragingly and promised to look into Singh's present relationship status. Tiana muttered to herself 'this act of love is too good to miss'. It meant that she wouldn't have to work hard on introducing them to each other or getting them to like each other. This was how she would fulfil the promise she had made to Ewaoluwa while in Nigeria.

Chapter Seven

BATON OF LOVE

On Monday 12th June 2018, Ewaoluwa began volunteering in Sanderstead Tiny Feet. The Littlewoods were very impressed with her outstanding performance and the level of expertise she displayed with all the children from crèche to reception. By Monday 25th June 2018, they had enrolled her for the teachers' exchange program. The program was a mentoring program that was aimed at equipping teachers in UK meet the teaching requirements of the present day child. In addition, teachers from European Union schools were invited to observe and see ways by which they could adopt the principles taught in the program and adapt it to fit their respective schools' needs around the globe. Ewaoluwa was the only African there. It was hosted by the Littlewoods but well attended by neighbouring infant and junior schools across UK.

LOVE ON SEPARATE GROUNDS

During the program, Ewaoluwa also thought about an all inclusive exchange program that would afford the school pupils from within UK interact with school pupils outside UK. She told Tiana and the Littlewoods about her ideas. They acknowledged its potency and Tiana was assigned the tasks of seeing how STF could incorporate it in their present teachers' exchange program. They would test run the pilot project on few ESGS pupils. The baton of love would thus be passed down from STF to ESGS. This would also involve supporting Ewaoluwa as she shuttled between Nigeria and UK. Tiana would also plan visits to ESGS to monitor their performance and look at what areas need to be improved on in the next program for teachers and children.

A couple of days after the program began, forty five year old Singh Raj bumped into Ewaoluwa again in the Freeman Garden. He seemed to be Ewaoluwa's ideal man with his good looks and well groomed body. He invited her for a walk in Freeman Garden and an evening outing afterwards. They both walked round the garden for about twenty minutes as she revelled herself in the scent of lavender. She began to fantasize again. It appeared that Singh Raj had received the command to love her from Singh Ghandi, some sort of baton and she was ready to receive the baton. She kept fantasizing about receiving a similar level of love Singh Ghandi had given her from Singh Raj. He reminded her of her late husband. By the end of the walk, she was really infatuated with the Indian man. It was as though Singh Ghandi had resurrected again.

They both left for Croham Park bed and breakfast. As they sat and drank some sours in the bar, Singh handed her a bouquet of roses and she thanked him. He steered at her for a prolonged time, admiring the new African beauty in Freeman Garden. Although he found her attractive, she was not as dark skinned as Tiana and she had beautiful dark skin and short curly hair. Her eyes were brown and beautiful and she had a pair of dimples which made her very cute. She had a fairly huge stature and was five feet six inches tall.

Singh told her that he came to Sanderstead ten years ago in response to the advert for a farm supervisor put up by Freeman Garden. Singh had studied agricultural economics in High Wycombe College and had gained managerial experience in garden shops. He got the job and rented a flat in Sanderstead. He became the farm manager after five years. He then asked her about her family. Ewaoluwa told Singh about her natal family and marriage to Singh Ghandi. She was quick to add that she was an exceptionally brilliant lady, with a masters degree in education. She also informed him that it was during her masters program that she met her three friends Tiana, Habiba and Chioma. The couple enjoyed each other's company for the rest of the evening. As the evening drew to a close, Singh walked Ewaoluwa back to Freeman cottage. He thanked Ewaoluwa once again and said that he had found her beautiful and would like to see her again. They bade each other farewell as Ewaoluwa retreated to her room in the Freeman's cottage.

As she lay on her bed, she thought of how lucky she was to have met Tiana and how lucky she was to have been given the opportunity of meeting Singh Raj. She felt he was also very courteous and the body chemistry present between them couldn't be missed. He called her later that night to thank her for the date and they both decided to spend their evenings together from then onwards till she returned to Nigeria.

However as she continued to live with the Freeman, she had to take up additional responsibilities which she never envisaged. With Alannah volunteering at the crèche, Tiana asked Ewaoluwa to help out with the children at home and also assist her with the administrative running of Freeman Home and Garden. This was apart from the voluntary role she was involved with at STF. The only task she was exempted from was that of the house keeper because Dahlia was responsible for that. Ewaoluwa began to resent Tiana, she felt all that Tiana did was issue commands to everyone in the home and garden. The teachers' exchange program was proving to be a cudgel set out to undermine Ewaoluwa's professionalism. Unlike the Littlewoods and

LOVE ON SEPARATE GROUNDS

Tiana, she was already an experienced teacher and a head teacher.

Two weeks into the program, Ewaoluwa fell out with Tiana. She felt that the presence of Singh Raj in her life meant that she didn't need to carry on with the laborious tasks in Freeman cottage. She had the mind to varnish with Singh like she had done at Fay's Sutton residence but she didn't want to miss out on the ongoing program. She hinted Singh Raj on the likelihood of her moving in with him, after complaining about the amount of work in Freeman cottage. Singh suggested that she moved out and rented a place like him. She took his advice and rented a room for two weeks. She thought that she would eventually prevail on Singh to allow her move in with him after the two weeks rent run out. She planned to make him the truncheon that would create mayhem in the life of Dr Oluiferiwa. Ewaoluwa then told Tiana that she was leaving for her own rented flat. Although Tiana was disappointed, she braved up to the news and let her go.

During the week, Ewaoluwa moved out, she called Singh and invited him to Nigeria. She wanted him to do business in Nigeria like Singh Ghandi had done. With Singh she was sure she would increase the influence she had in Nigeria. She told him that she wanted to offer him the best of life in Nigeria and he said that he would think about it. Shortly after she moved out of Freeman Cottage, she noticed that Singh drifted away from her quietly and when she confronted him, he said he wasn't interested in her anymore.

She sought to find the reason for his sudden pull away and change of attitude towards her. He told her that though he loved her, she had fallen out of favour with Tiana and the Freeman household. She asked him what he meant by that and said that she thought he had advised her to move out so they could spend more time together. She then asked him what he meant by saying that he loved her because of Tiana. He responded by saying that her falling out with Tiana was no good to him; he needed her favour and Jayden's to continue with his job. He apologised and told her that it's the way life worked. Ewaoluwa couldn't believe her ears. To her that meant that she had lost the staff of authority that she had over Tiana and the Littlewoods.

Despite all persuasions that she wouldn't let their relationship get in the way of his work for Freeman Garden, Singh refused to move the relationship forward nor would he succumb to her pleas. She inquired about the parameters he used to gauge the love he once felt for her and he insisted that Tiana was the reason why he wanted a relationship with her. He then said in a cynical manner that he had hoped to rise above Tiana, deputise Jayden and join him in running the affairs of the Home and Garden. He believed Jayden should be in charge not Tiana. On hearing this, Ewaoluwa confided in him that she also needed him in her life to act as a weapon to destroy Dr Oluiferiwa.

After that conversation, she never heard from Singh again. He avoided her in Sanderstead and having left the Freeman cottage, he was out of her reach there too. Ewaoluwa was once again shattered emotionally. She couldn't face the financial implications of her decision to rent an accommodation alone for the next six weeks. There was no where to loan money from neither was there anyone willing to loan her money. She had to return to Nigeria unannounced. That was the end of her participation in the program for the year. She then planned to take out her revenge on the two men who had used her and dumped her; Dr Oluiferiwa and Singh Raj.

She arrived in Nigeria sooner than expected to the amazement of her staff and the trustees. She said that although the program was still on, she didn't think that ESGS was prepared for the program that year. It was the pilot scheme and they hadn't been well briefed on the financial implications and program requirements. She told them that she had gained little exposure from the brief period she spent at the program and the knowledge she had acquired, if implemented in ESGS in the next one year, would be enough for the year. Back in her flat, Ewaoluwa once again planned to settle down to running ESGS. By then she was very angry at life and bitterness had corroded her heart. She couldn't control herself. It appeared that she was losing all she had at every opportunity that came her way.

On her way back from church one Sunday afternoon, she got into her car to drive away but heard a familiar voice behind her call her name. She turned around and saw Habiba; she was with the senate president of Nigeria and a young lady. Ewaoluwa got down from the car and went over to greet them as well as embrace Habiba. She said that she was truly pleased to see her. Habiba introduced the lady beside her as Phillippa Mansir; her sixteen year old step daughter. The man with her was her brother in law; Khatumu Mansir; the senate president. Ewaoluwa acknowledged seeing and hearing about the senate president on the news but didn't know he was related to Habiba. She then told Ewaoluwa that her husband Safiyanu had found a job as a project analyst in Windsor and had relocated shortly after their marriage in 2017. Habiba would be joining him in August 2018 with Phillippa who was going for her A-levels program. Ewaoluwa exchanged pleasantries with them and suggested they all went for a drink in the chapel's café.

However Khatumu volunteered to take Phillippa to the shopping mall instead so the two friends could spend some time together. He promised Habiba that he would come back for her later and asked her to call him when she was ready to leave. Habiba and Ewaoluwa then retreated to the chapel's café to have a drink. Fortunately

LOVE ON SEPARATE GROUNDS

Ewaoluwa didn't have a program lined up for the afternoon.

The two friends chatted for a while before Habiba raised the issue of her relationship with Tiana. Habiba said that she had heard the rumour that Tiana volunteered to help Ewaoluwa in UK but the two of them had embarrassed themselves in the midst of an international educational program, to the dismay of their host and hostess. She said that she also heard that they had both fallen out over an Indian man. Habiba said that she couldn't confirm the story because there was a lot of distortion in it. She knew Tiana was already married to Jayden so she couldn't be contending with Ewaoluwa over an Indian man. At least the last she knew, Tiana was happily married to Jayden. She then asked Ewaoluwa to confirm the story.

Ewaoluwa was shocked when she heard Habiba's version of the story. She then explained to Habiba that the reason for the fall out was due to the unreasonable demands placed on her by Tiana and her family. She felt that the amount of responsibilities thrust on her by Tiana was getting in the way of her personal life. She insinuated that with Tiana, there was no free personal time; she was either looking after the children at home or looking after them in the nursery. The only free personal time she had in the house was the time that she got into her bed and slept at night. Habiba chuckled but said nothing.

Ewaoluwa admitted to striking it off with an Indian guy; one of the men working for Freeman Garden and having a relationship with him. She said that the relationship was brief because the time she should have invested in it was what Tiana had demanded from her. Tiana's expectations bit into her personal time. She allured to the fact that the bone of contention was really Tiana and her demands. Habiba nodded her head in an acknowledgement that showed that she understood what Ewaoluwa had just said.

Habiba said that she was sorry that Ewaoluwa's relationship with Singh didn't work out. Ewaoluwa responded by saying that it was God's way of exposing Singh's deception and went further to inform Habiba of Singh's plan to depose Tiana. Ewaoluwa was also quick to add that she had been the one protecting Tiana from her contending staff who felt that Jayden should be in charge not her. Suddenly Ewaoluwa had an idea of how to get rid of Singh Raj. She decided to secretely plan how to use Habiba as the shillelagh to get rid of Singh Raj. It would be a quiet plot.

Habiba on the other hand said that she was disappointed in Ewaoluwa and Tiana but she believed that to save the day, Ewaoluwa should apologise to Tiana. She had more to gain from the relationship than Tiana had to lose. She prevailed over Ewaoluwa and Ewaoluwa agreed that an apology was in order. She said she was sorry for what she did and promised to give Tiana a call after Habiba had spoken to her.

Furthermore, Ewaoluwa said that she believed her right had been trampled upon and she felt betrayed. She said that although Tiana knew she was more experienced than her, she wanted her to come and submit to her because she was in UK. She also said that she felt bitter because it was through her connections in Nigeria that Tiana got her teaching experience. It was also Ewaoluwa that showed her the ropes of teaching in Nigeria. It was through Ewaoluwa's teaching agency that Tiana got her first set of pupils she took in private tuition when she was pregnant and needed to augment her income. She literally trained Tiana in Nigeria. Tiana knew she was a head teacher, running her own school in Nigeria, yet she and her white friends wanted to exploit her in UK by asking her to come down and accept the role of a teaching assistant during the teachers' exchange program.

In addition, Ewaoluwa said that she would have tolerated the situation for the short period if Tiana didn't move the goal post in her home. Tiana had made her nanny, Alannah a nursery assistant because she was Irish and turned her; a trained head teacher to a nanny at home. She also accused Tiana of making her do some administrative tasks in Freeman Garden. She claimed that when

LOVE ON SEPARATE GROUNDS

Tiana approached her about the opportunity initially, she told her that she didn't need to do anything at home as her parents-in-law had a house keeper to look after the house, a nanny to look after the children and staff to look after the garden. Habiba sympathised with Ewaoluwa but insisted that her apology was the path to reconciliation and progress. It was almost six o'clock in the evening when Khatumu called. Habiba said she was ready to leave and he came to pick her up. She left promising to speak with Tiana that evening.

Later in the day, Habiba communicated Ewaoluwa's apology to Tiana and raised all the issues she had discussed with her. Tiana thanked Habiba for intervening. She responded by saying that she was very disappointed in Ewaoluwa and her disposition as she remembered all that had transpired between them. Tiana had helped her get into the UK system, housed her and even introduced her to a responsible man whom she and Jayden felt had bright future prospects. Tiana said that she was going to hand her loyal, dedicated and hardworking farm manager; Singh Raj to Ewaoluwa on a platter of gold but she had blown it.

She reminded Habiba that she didn't receive Jayden on a platter of gold. They all knew the price she had to pay. Tiana continued by saying that in return for her kind acts, Ewaoluwa had left her stranded with the Littlewoods, abandoned her at home with her children and humiliated her in her parents in-law's home. They had opened their doors to her, fed and accommodated her at no cost but she had abused the hospitality.

Tiana reiterated on the fact that she really felt betrayed by Ewaoluwa's actions. She said that after her sudden departure, the Littlewoods conducted further background checks on her. They found out to their amazement that despite the front she put up as an experienced and seasoned professional, she had a previous record of misconduct with the educational board in UK and had been suspended from teaching for a number of years. The grapevine had it that she had done something similar a while back when she was hosted by her cousin Fay and her husband in Sutton. She had disappointed them, gone off with an Indian man and finally got caught up with substance abuse, which eventually led to the misconduct.

According to Tiana, the only consolation that the Littlewoods had was that the incidence had taken place about sixteen years earlier so they could argue the case with the education board if challenged. They knew sixteen years was more than enough to reinstate a petty offender, if she was repentant. To the best of their knowledge, Ewaoluwa had been repentant within the UK and European jurisdiction. Habiba expressed her shock at the revelations that Tiana had disclosed about Ewaoluwa. She was sure that if she had lived with them while they were still in school, they would have found out all the facts from her previous life. Ewaoluwa was the only one who came to school from home; the three others had lived together in their rented Onike apartment.

In addition, Habiba went on to further disclose Ewaoluwa's drug entanglement in Nigeria, her involvement with Singh Ghandi and how she almost lost ESGS. Tiana shook her head in disbelief. Habiba also informed Tiana that she also heard of Ewaoluwa's likely involvement with the drug saga at Pansy's Chest a couple of months back. Although there was no tangible evidence to indict her, Ewaoluwa's close buddy; Alfred was a high suspect. It appeared they were dating then and she was frequently seen in his Ikeja residence. Also many of Alfred's close allies formed the cartel in the recreation cluster of Pansy's Chest.

The two friends nodded their heads in disbelief at how Ewaoluwa had turned out. It seemed to both Habiba and Tiana that Ewaoluwa had an agreement with the drug house, that if she ever got disappointed, the drug house was where to go. The two friends chuckled, but were dismayed. Tiana buttressed on the point that she expected more from Ewaoluwa than she got. She had brought Ewaoluwa from Nigeria into her marital home, cared for her, got her a good job and even linked her up with a potential suitor. In the end, like the proverbial leopard that doesn't change her spots, she betrayed her. She said that she and Jayden were fortunate that Freeman Garden still had Singh Raj. Her parents' in law would have been very angry and disappointed with them if they had interfered with Singh's job as he ran the Freeman Garden. Tiana felt it was rather unfortunate that Ewaoluwa betrayed the people that cared for her the most.

However Habiba prevailed on Tiana and she agreed to reconcile with Ewaoluwa, if she tendered an apology to her and her family as well as the Littlewoods. What Tiana couldn't promise was the likelihood of reinstating Ewaoluwa's integrity with the Littlewoods. She had missed a vital part of the teachers' exchange program that year and all that was left was the children's exchange program. It would take the special grace of God for the Littlewoods to agree to sign up ESGS pupils, as the program was scheduled to begin in a forth night. Friday 3rd August 2018.

Chapter Eight

HELMET OF LOVE

Habiba got in touch with Ewaoluwa and gave her the feedback from the phone conversation with Tiana. She reminded her of the need to apologise urgently and ask for a recall of ESGS's slot in the ongoing program. They had lost the slot when Ewaoluwa fell out with Tiana and the Littlewoods, who had acted as a cover to protect her in the teaching profession. Habiba was the mediator of the reconciliation so she got Ewaoluwa to apologise to all the parties that she had disappointed in UK. She also got her to make a vow to be of good conduct and stay off drugs. Habiba also rebuked her for thinking drugs was the way out of life's challenges. It seemed her feet were quicker to go to the drug house than to go to a counselling unit like Pansy's Chest or even Mercy Chapel. Habiba cynically said that Lady Davina had made herself available to Ewaoluwa but it appeared that she was obviously not programmed for divine counselling.

LOVE ON SEPARATE GROUNDS

On tendering the apology to all concerned, they all accepted Ewaoluwa but the Littlewoods were sorry she couldn't be drafted into the teacher's exchange program for the year. They pointed out that it was their maiden edition; an international event and their sponsors had been taken aback at Ewaoluwa's sudden departure. She knew that she was the only African there yet she left unceremoniously. They however suggested the possibility of enrolling her in the following year, if she was still interested. It was subject to the approval of the planning committee who acted like medieval armour for them at the education board.

However they hinted that she may be allowed to enrol ESGS pupils. That was the only option opened to her at the moment and she was lucky because it was her brain child and Tiana was in charge. Tiana insisted that Habiba signed an undertaking as a guarantor to be responsible for Ewaoluwa in UK. Habiba agreed and Ewaoluwa was then given the invitation to bring in ESGS children. Shortly after this, Habiba then left Nigeria with Phillippa to join her husband in UK. After spending about two weeks in Nigeria, Tiana arranged with Ewaoluwa to bring her pupils to the exchange program hosted by Tiana and the Littlewoods in Sanderstead Tiny Feet. She had just about a week to announce to the parents of ESGS pupils. Only four parents were able to respond to the invitation and commit financially within the short notice period given. These would represent ESGS in the program in UK in the last week of August 2018.

Although they would be living in the Freeman cottage, all their events would be held in STF premises. A coach would be hired for the entire week to take them from Freeman cottage to STF and other places arranged for them to visit. The Littlewoods promised to observe the events and if it had potentials for success, they would incorporate it in the teacher's exchange program the following year. They felt it maybe a good way to wrap up the teachers' exchange program annually.

Ewaoluwa took the four children from ESGS who were between the ages of six to ten to Freeman cottage on Saturday 25th August 2018. Jayden was pleased to see her again though she was silently ashamed of her past and how she left him and Tiana stranded as she went off with Singh Raj, who later jilted her. Only the thought of revenge would comfort her and make up for the loss, so she braved the moment and put up a front. She had launched her first attack on Dr Praise O'Figbayemi and that had created a rippling effect on his highly esteemed family.

She promised herself that the next attack would be launched on Singh Raj and the final one would be targeted at the source of her pain; Dr Oluiferiwa. To achieve this she was going to purposely seek out a wealthy and influential politician, marry him, climb the political ladder and secretly get back at him. Her plan for Singh Raj was to get him sacked from Freeman Garden and send him into penury and despondency. Then she would have been avenged of all her foes. The very thought was so appealing to her morale.

She then remembered Habiba and the senator. Habiba had travelled out with her step daughter to join her husband in UK. Yes the Nigerian senate president would be okay for her. He would be a more efficient shillelagh than Habiba. Her plan was then to try and get to the senator through Habiba. She had been so lost in thought that she didn't hear Tiana until she tapped her on the shoulder.

Tiana informed Ewaoluwa that before she arrived, she had planned with Habiba that they go on a week end away. They would be visiting Habiba and her family in Windsor on that same day. This was part of the reconciliatory plan to ensure Ewaoluwa knew what was at stake if she messed up. The six months Freeman twins, Chrysan and Marie and the four ESGS pupils were left in the care of Alannah and Rita, while Tiana and Ewaoluwa went off to see Habiba in Windsor. They travelled by train.

On getting to Windsor, they agreed to meet up for a meal at the restaurant and have a reunion to talk things through. Habiba seemed

LOVE ON SEPARATE GROUNDS

to have settled down well. She was able to rent a commercial space where she ran another restaurant in Windsor. Neither Tiana nor Habiba had heard from Chioma.

Tiana said that the last time she has heard from Chioma was when she came for her baby shower and wedding at Freeman Cottage. Although they sent her a thank you card, both she and Jayden hadn't been able to visit her in Birmingham. She had informed them that she was engaged and In addition, they spoke extensively about what had transpired between Tiana and Ewaoluwa. Habiba appealed to Ewaoluwa that she had signed an undertaking for her in UK and would be grateful if she was of good conduct. She told her that she was also expected to comport herself well in front of the Littlewoods and planning committee for the program, as well as Tiana's family and the Garden staff. Both Habiba and Tiana said that they were sorry that things didn't work out well between Ewaoluwa and Singh Raj.

More so Habiba assured her that God would bring her the perfect match in good time, someone that would complement her. Habiba further said that Ewaoluwa had a big cap that only a man with a big head can wear. That meant that she had to wait for the one whose head would fit the size of her cap. According to her, Singh Raj may seem like her prince in shining armour but from the little she had heard about him, his head was too small for her cap.

LOVE ON SEPARATE GROUNDS

She reckoned that Singh had a baby's head that would be lost in her big cap. Ewaoluwa chuckled, thanked them and reassured both that she would adhere to the advice.

The three friends then made their way to the Guild Hall where they saw portraits and artefacts that shed more light on Britain. Then they went to the market where Ewaoluwa got souvenirs for the Parents of ESGS pupils. Next they decided to go on the river bus which took off firstly on the roads of Windsor before cruising into the waters. The tour guide gave a brief description of the town. By eight o'clock in the evening, Habiba invited them for dinner in her home.

Exhausted, the ladies retreated to Habiba's Victorian residence on Victoria Street and her husband Safiyanu opened the door. The ladies went to the dinner table as Phillippa served a three course meal. The starter was smoked salmon with Irish soda bread, woodland sorrel and cress, the main meal was marshed potatoes with greens and the dessert was yoghurt. Habiba was quick to tell her guests that Phillippa had prepared the meals, she was presently being trained as a chef in a restaurant and she was also starting her A-levels program in September 2018. Habiba and Tiana thanked Phillippa and told her that they were proud of her and wished her success in her studies and career path. They hoped Philippa and Habiba made a good team with the restaurant.

LOVE ON SEPARATE GROUNDS

Safiyanu was so good at cracking jokes that he made them laugh throughout their meal and later jokingly accused them of bad table manners. He told them he was glad the ladies had turned up, if they hadn't, he would have divorced Habiba on the basis of cheating on him. Tiana asked why he thought so and he responded by saying that the last time Habiba prepared intensely for any outing was a day before their wedding. He claimed that only her female friends or a secret lover could have made Habiba prepare and dress the way she did before meeting up with them that day. The ladies smiled and teased Habiba suggesting that her glamour and elegance were getting extinct in Mansirs' home.

A while later Jayden called Tiana to let her know that he had missed her and would be spending the night in front of the computer. He told her that Alannah and Rita had managed the twins and the four ESGS pupils well. They had been fed and tucked into bed after watching a children's movie. Tiana thanked Rita and Alannah and they both left for their respective homes. Tiana told Jay that she had missed him too but was too tired to stay awake for a chat. After dinner, Ewaoluwa and Tiana thanked their hosts and retreated to bed.

While in bed, Ewaoluwa grew envious of both Tiana and Habiba. They were settled in a happy union in UK, Tiana had their own children and Habiba was few months pregnant. She on the other hand was stuck with a failed relationship and a mission to revenge. All forms of protective authoritative covering had been stripped off her.

Then she remembered the reason for coming to see Habiba and her family. She was going to use what she had to move close to him at all cost. She knew that Habiba and Safiyanu would be the best link to get to Khatumu. Now she was prepared to be a seventh wife, if she had to. Khatumu was powerful enough for her; he would provide the much needed covering that would love her and fight for her. A helmet of love she would wear to victory as she gave her mission the best shot. Nothing was going to stop her now. With this thought, she drifted to bed.

The next morning they sat down to a breakfast of cereal, toast and tea before setting out for Windsor castle. It was past noon when Safiyanu took his family and guests and headed for the castle, where they took a tour round. The splendour of the colossal edifice was breathtaking. The fortification of the external envelope was beyond the imagination of the modern child as it was hard to imagine the extent the ancient monarchy went to guarantee their safety in war times. Next they observed the changing of the guards and it was as captivating as the guards were immaculately dressed. They also carried out the task in a breath taking manner.

LOVE ON SEPARATE GROUNDS

Next they headed for St George's chapel, this was another architectural edifice within Windsor Castle. The degree of accuracy with which each individual element was brought together to form the magnificent interior layout provoked worship to a supreme God whose excellence was beyond human comprehension. They were told that the Queen worshipped there when she was around and it was also opened to the public during service times. They had missed the morning service.

They then proceeded to the grand reception room. This room was so magnificent that it depicted what affluence meant to the ordinary mind. The galleries within the castle were so glamorous that it gave a minute glimpse of what the biblical King Solomon's palace might have been like. The state apartments and semi state rooms were so nicely presented that it was impossible not to feel like a royal as one went from one room to the next. The treasures of the castle were so neatly presented that it succinctly captured the British history with minimal portraits and antiques. Ewaoluwa expressed so much joy at what she was seeing; saying that every teacher that goes to UK must visit the castle. The experience was better imagined than told. She and Tiana thanked Safiyanu and Habiba for the outing.

Finally, they all went back to the Mansirs' Victorian residence where Habiba and her family hosted Tiana and Ewaoluwa to lunch at home. Phillippa once again prepared butternut squash apple and roast turkey salad. During lunch, a phone call came through for Safiyanu but it was Habiba that picked it up. It was Khatumu Mansir, the senate president. He was in UK and would be stopping by to see his brother and the family. Habiba passed the phone to Safiyanu who apologised for not informing her sooner. Khatumu had arrived the previous day and called to say that he would be coming over for lunch. As they ate lunch, Khatumu walked in and joined the table. Luckily Philippa had made a bit more than enough to go round so there was enough for him to eat. Khatumu said he was glad to see Ewaoluwa once again.

Although he was in his sixties, Khatumu still looked handsome and vibrant. Ewaoluwa blushed when he greeted her. He told her that he remembered dropping Habiba off at Mercy Chapel's café a few weeks back. He hadn't expected to see Ewaoluwa in Habiba's home in UK; however he was glad to see her again. He then turned to Tiana and said that he was swept off his feet by Tiana's beauty. He soon began flattering her and he finally asked her out. Tiana smiled as she became slightly embarrassed. The atmosphere got tense and Habiba quickly moved in to rescue the situation. Habiba informed him that they were all married. Ewaoluwa's heart sank as she became devastated. What was Habiba playing at? She wasn't married and had even told Habiba about her failed relationships prior to that day. She felt Habiba was being mean or just trying to prevent her from meeting Khatumu. She began to feel some disdain for Habiba. She made up her mind to get through to Khatumu that afternoon, even if her actions ended the friendship with Tiana and Habiba.

However Khatumu looked at Habiba, grinned and told her to mind her business. He turned again to Tiana, shook her hands and told her that he was married too. Tiana relaxed and told him that he looked good and that she was glad to have met the Nigerian senate president. She further went ahead and said that Habiba didn't disclose that they had such a noble personality in the family she was marrying into when she got married. At that point, Habiba interrupted them and told Khatumu that if he wanted another feather to his cap, he could try Ewaoluwa. This embarrassed Ewaoluwa, who by now had mixed feelings about the lunch. Up till then, she had enjoyed their company. Khatumu smiled and looked at Tiana as she looked away. He then faced Ewaoluwa, took off his bowler hat and bowed to her. He then smiled and said 'we learn that you ma'am are married and available, well so am I'. The room went silent again. Ewaoluwa was speechless as the spotlight hit her. She blushed and Khatumu continued his chat. He told her that he had three wives and nine children. His third wife lived with him and their son in Nigerian. The other two lived in UK and USA respectively, each with her four children.

This disappointed Ewaoluwa further; in reality he had more than one wife and if she became his, she would be number four. She then told them that she was widowed. He held out his hand towards her and apologised for having being insensitive. Ewaoluwa told him that Singh Ghandi had passed away eleven years before. Safiyanu said 'Oh it's more than enough time for you to grief; I thought it was recent, because it appears you had been grieving since you got in here'. Habiba then cautioned him and he apologised.

Safiyanu told his brother that he heard that Ewaoluwa had just come out of a rough relationship with an Indian guy and that was why he teased her. He wanted her to open her heart once again to love. Singh was just one man amidst millions on earth. Ewaoluwa smiled at this point, she was really short of words. Her line of thoughts had been distorted and she didn't know what to say. It was as though the lunch had been held in her honour and it was her turn to give the vote of thanks or response.

She soon regained her composure, smiled and told them that she was grateful for the amount of knowledge that she would be taking back to Nigeria. She also told them about her work as a teacher, her present involvement with the children's exchange program in UK and how much interest she had in politics. She told them of how her former boyfriend Oluiferiwa had encouraged her in politics too before they parted. Back in her mind, she vowed that she was going to give all it took to marry this very rich and influential politician in government. Then she would go back and befriend Oluiferiwa and his family, position them in strategic places from soldiers on foot to presidency. She must have every one of his friends, from the legislative council to the executive and from the judiciary arms to the presidency. She must have them all and Khatumu seemed to be the right helmet that fitted the role she desperately needed.

'You seem to be in another planet, Ewaar'? She heard Khatumu say. She was shocked and there was tremor in her voice. 'No ….. err …… just thinking of how handsome you looked, sir'. She heard herself say. Oh dear, she had been lost in her thinking. 'Would you like to meet up with me again, Ewaar'? She was shocked once more. Ewaar? No one calls her that. Khatumu said again 'Ewaar, what got you thinking'? She quickly regained her posture and said 'I would love to support your party in the forth coming elections next year, sir'. Oh no, she thought to herself. What had she just done, she thought? She must be silly to have spoken out like that. Now the guy would think that she was desperate. She felt really sore and sorry.

'Okay dear, here is my card. Give me a call when you are ready for a chat'. Ewaoluwa took the card but said nothing. 'By the way when are you returning to Nigeria'? She told him that she was there for only a week before she returned with the children. After lunch, Tiana and Ewaoluwa thanked the Mansirs before boarding the train back to Sanderstead.

On their way back, the two friends agreed that the visit to Windsor had changed their perspective of holidays in UK. Ewaoluwa confirmed that in all her years in UK, she only went to night clubs, eateries, parties, and places of worship, she had also visited friends. They both agreed that it was a good idea to visit places of interest during the holidays. They had just experienced a brilliant week end away and looked forward to taking the children out during the week.

Prior to now, Tiana had never been anywhere but Bournemouth, where they spent their honeymoon. She and her husband had agreed to postpond it until after the birth of the twins earlier in the year. At the time of her arrival in UK late last year, she was heavily pregnant and she didn't have any desire to travel far. The week end outing meant a lot to her because she was with her friends. Ewaoluwa was silently grateful for the luck of meeting Khatumu. She was still thinking of how she would get his details off Habiba and meet up with him in Nigeria. Now all the details were handed down to her on a platter of gold. Ewaoluwa and Tiana arrived in Sanderstead late at night. They were the only ones awake in the cottage so they had their showers and went to bed.

Chapter Nine

BANNER OF LOVE

Back in Freeman cottage, Tiana and the Littlewoods planned to take Ewaoluwa and her pupils to different places of interest under the banner of STF camp. There were twelve other pupils from STF that joined the children's exchange program, all ages between six and ten years old too. The hired coach went to pick the Littlewoods and Tiana's team from their homes daily before heading to the pick up point which was STF premise. The pupils who weren't local residents were encouraged to spend the week with their friends who lived locally. These twenty two individuals made up the STF camp.

On Monday, the STF camp was welcomed to the program by the Littlewoods who told them what to expect and what was expected of them. They then thanked the children for turning up and introduced a game that offered everyone the opportunity to introduce themselves and learn one another's names. It was then time to begin their trip so all the children given their pack lunches and guided into the coach.

They visited the Battersea Park Children's Zoo. ESGS pupils saw different animals and admitted that they had never heard of some of them before their visit. The younger children had their faces painted while the older ones went to the mask making section, Where face masks were made for each of them to take away. They were also allowed to go on the amusement rides and see the life sized helicopter and fire engine as well as the tractor. They then settled down and had their pack lunch, which was mainly fruits and water. Next they headed to the London Aquarium. The children all found the underwater aquarium with its sea life fascinating. The day's outing ended with lunch at McDonalds. At the three places the children had taken group pictures with their teachers, they were all really excited and grateful to their teachers.

Ewaoluwa called Khatumu in the evening to have a chat and apologise for the poor finishing at Habiba's place. Khatumu responded that he understood the pain she felt, seeing she had just come out of a failed relationship and needed time to bounce back. She learnt that Khatumu had studied in the UK and got married quite young.

His first wife, Zubaydah was born and bred in the UK, although she was originally from Plateau State, Nigeria. The marriage had produced four children but she told him that she couldn't live permanently in Nigeria. The four sons were all living and working in UK. She insisted on staying back with her children. Through Khatumu's business contacts, he met his second wife, Fa'iqah in US. They got married and she also had four children who lived in US. His two daughters and two sons in US had also nationalised there. Being a business woman, Fa'iqah was a frequent traveller, so she was hardly at home to take care of him. She insisted on keeping her children in the US.

However over the years, the consequences of his two wives' choices left him exposed to his female servants in Nigeria. He did confess that in times past, he had intimacy with his female servants but decided to stop when Khadijah came. She was brought into the house to assist him at a tender age of sixteen. Her parents could not afford her school fees so they sent her to him to train and marry her. He then changed all his female staff and sent Khadijah to study education in Abuja Teacher's Training College. This was while he was working in the ministry in Abuja. They both had a son together named Shamshudeen.

Although the two wives lived with their children overseas, they were encouraged to visit Khatumu in Nigeria once a year since he had supported all of them financially and had ensured he played a fatherly role to them in UK and US respectively. His presence was felt in their homes as he made it a duty to constantly visit them whenever he was outside the country. Khatumu's house in Nigeria was always a full house when his two wives and eight children joined him, Khadijah and Shamshudeen for the muslim festival in August when he held an annual feast that year. This was also the time Shamshudeen saw all his siblings. Khatumu said he had flown into London straight after hosting his family to the annual feast.

Khadijah frequently visits her eighteen years old son, Shamshudeen in a boarding school in Abuja. He had warned Khadijah that he wouldn't allow Shashudeen to study outside the country so he could have a son nearby. During the holidays, Khadijah taught her son at home to ensure he was up to scratch with his studies. The sixty two years old Khatumu said he loved Shamsudeen most, out of his nine children because he was a very kind and humble boy. He was also very quiet and hardworking.

According to Khatumu, Shamshudeen was allowed frequent travels within and outside the country because he wanted him to be enlightened enough to run the business at home, as well as get involved with politics on his graduation from the university. He was always accompanied by his mother when he travelled. 'Oh dear, Khatumu had a band of army in his camp already', Ewaoluwa thought to herself. She had to decide if she wanted to add to the number, seeing that she desired to have her own children too. She teased him by saying that he could have a foot ball team and host a match during his annual August feast. He asked her why she thought so and she stated that the eleven people in his conjugal family already made the number. He acknowledged her sense of humour and teasingly said that he expected more children from her, so they can have reserves too. Then she would be a player and he would be the referee.

Once again Ewaoluwa had found a banner in her search for love. This banner was the Mansirs and it was all she needed to execute her revenge on Oluiferiwa; the source of all her pain. She only hoped that she would succeed with the Mansirs. This is about the best opportunity she can get and if she missed it, she would have lost everything; she may be as good as dead. She then remembered that she had to instigate Singh's removal before she left UK. She didn't hear the last bit of what Khatumu had said until he bade her goodnight because she had been lost in her thoughts. He hung up the phone before she had the chance to ask him any questions. She knew at that point that she had to try and remain focused whenever she was with him.

The next day, they gathered at STF again for the day's welcome address and briefing by the Littlewoods. As the coach took the STF camp to Brighton beach, the children were encouraged to interact with one another. It was an exciting day for all as the weather was really cool. They all had their pack lunch on the beach, which had marshed potatoes with greens and sausages. They also had some fruits and a bottle of water. Next they played different games and later danced to some music from the music box they took to the beach. They were later allowed to play by the shoreline before heading back to Sanderstead.

Khatumu called Ewaoluwa again at night time. They chatted well into the night and having found that they got on so well, he invited her out the next day. On Wednesday, Ewaoluwa told the Littlewoods that she would be joining the team later because she had to meet up with one of ESGS trustees. She dared not tell them that it was a potential lover. While she waited behind for Khatumu, the STF camp went to the local library after their breakfast before proceeding to Beddington park to play and have lunch. While the children were away, Khatumu came to take Ewaoluwa out.

As they stepped out of Freeman cottage, she saw a toyota prius plug-in hybrid packed on the adjacent street. Khatumu led her to the car and she was godsmack, the car looked expensive and classy. She didn't believe it was his car, though she knew he was very rich. It seemed all the men she dated recently had really smashing cars. He was staying with one of his sons in his Mayfair apartment in London but he was able to drive down to get her to Beddington Park.

LOVE ON SEPARATE GROUNDS

They later joined the STF camp where the Littlewoods engaged all the children in the park. Wallington brought nostalgic memories to Ewaoluwa, she couldn't say that she was proud of her achievements when she was there; neither would she say that she is proud to be Khatumu's fourth wife now but her passion for revenge on Oluiferiwa was so chronic that she was determined to marry Khatumu.

At the park, on enquiring about her expectations from a relationship, Ewaoluwa said that she just wanted acceptance from the man she was going to marry, she wanted to love and be loved in return and she was hoped to have children in the marriage. She told him that she also had the ambition to be the first lady in Nigeria and hoped he had the ambition to fly with her wings of support. She then said regrettably that she had wished Oluiferiwa was a bit more caring and considerate but she also blamed her temperament. Khatumu chuckled. 'So if I dare misbehave Ewaar, I would be beaten up too', he asked with an enquiry look? 'Yes babes, you would be beaten to a pulp with a three mouthed horse whip, strapped to a horse back and sent back to Abuja, where you came from' was her response. Then she went ahead to say she was sorry she acted in that manner to Dr Oluiferiwa and had regretted the action. Khatumu smiled once again and told her that he wanted someone to take care of him in the house as Khadijah devoted time to her son in Abuja.

Ewaoluwa assured him that she would love to look after him. She told him that Dr Oluiferiwa considered her to be very caring and compassionate, despite her aggressive approach to life. In the evening, the STF camp went to Trafalgar Square where they saw and fed the birds there. They also took pictures before going to visit Madame Tussauds, where they watched an animated film.

Khatumu volunteered to take Tiana in his car. Afterwards the coach took the STF camp back to Freeman cottage while Khatumu took Ewaoluwa to Croham Park for a drink of strawberry smoothes. He finally dropped her at the Freeman cottage. By the time Ewaoluwa got to Freeman cottage, Jayden and Tiana were hosting all the kids and their parents to a night of games and pizza with ice cream. They all slept on the floor in the living room. Grandpa George and Grandma Rose were both happy for the exciting company they had received that day.

On Thursday, the children woke up late due to the late night of games. After the last child had been cleaned up and dressed, their parents thanked the Freemans and left. The STF camp then went to Windsor, where they visited legoland. The children went on the rides, took lots of pictures and also bought souvenirs for their parents from their pocket money. Everyone came back really exhausted. They had an early dinner and went off to sleep. On Friday, after breakfast, the STF camp met at the school for a session with the Littlewoods. The children were encouraged to continue with their good behaviour, work hard at school and help their parents at home. Bryce told them about sustainability and the need to take good care of everything they were given. Alexia stressed on the importance of them maintaining good hygiene. She also told them that she expected them to work so hard so that they can be great leaders in the future. Alexia told them that was the only way they can help their parents in return for the wonderful things they receive.

After the school session, they were scheduled to visit Freeman Garden next. Tiana asked Singh Raj to take the STF camp on a tour round the garden and the children were really excited to see the myriad of flowers and animals in the garden. Then they had an outdoor picnic in rear lawn of the cottage. They were also allowed to play in the oval pool for about half an hour before heading to Sanderstead market where they had the opportunity to be part of the village's annual funfair. That was the end of the day's event.

Memories of Ewaoluwa's early years in UK flooded through her mind. She had so many life regrets which was the reason she was adamant on executing the revenge planned against Oluiferiwa. She wanted him to pay for all the misfortunes that had come her way. She was going to use him as her proverbial scapegoat, seeing that he had been the worst of the lot that dated, used and dumped her. On Saturday, the STF camp went to Chessington world of adventures, where they went on the different rides and also had the opportunity to see other animals. They had fun at the theme park and came back really excited. Finally, the coach dropped the STF camp at their school premise. The Littlewoods thanked all the children for coming and hoped they all had a good outing with them. The children all responded in the affirmative and promised to encourage their parents to allow them continue with the exchange program annually.

Rita then announced that the pupils from Sanderstead Tiny Feet had gifts to give to everyone. The head girl, Mercedes Sheerwood came forward, thanked everyone for the exciting outing and presented each of them with a tiny palm sized solar panel lamp. She told them that she heard from her geography class that there is a lot of sunshine in Nigeria. She told them that the tiny lamps were solar panel lamps which could be recharged with sunlight, rather than batteries. She then urged them to go and be a light to the world in their respective schools. This was followed by a round of applause. Next Alannah said that the ESGS pupils also had gifts to present to everyone. The head boy for

ESGS, Gbopemioluwa Oluseohuntutun stepped forward and thanked every one for making their stay enjoyable. He told them that they should continue to be good pupils that their teachers and parents would be proud of. He then said that they would let their parents in Nigeria know about the solar panel lamps and the benefits of conserving energy, looking after themselves and maintaining a healthy environment. Then was also followed by another round of applause as the four ESGS pupils presented each person with an A-4 sized handcrafted leather folder from Northern Nigeria.

Ewaoluwa thanked all the organisers and the children for making the vision a reality. That outing marked the end of the children exchange program. The parents in UK all came to pick up their children while the coach dropped Tiana and her team at Freeman cottage. They got back early enough for dinner and encouraged the children to go to bed, so they could leave for the airport early the next day.

On Sunday morning, the Freeman household and their guests had breakfast together and the children were all full of thanks and appreciation to the Tiana and Ewaoluwa. The children presented Tiana and her family with gifts. They gave Grandma George a nicely decorated wooden calabash, cleverly woven from the eastern part of Nigeria. They presented Jayden and George with men's traditional cap, made from aso-oke from Sagamu, where Tiana grew up. They gave Tiana and Ewaoluwa automatic head gears which was of similar fabrics as the traditional caps. They also presented George and Rose Freeman with a large African canvass painting of the palace at Ile Ife, the cradle of Yoruba people and gave the six month old twins two small wooden rattles and two small sized talking drum nicely crafted from the north.

The head boy, Gbopemioluwa gave the vote of thanks. Jay was moved to tears at the children's response and so he wrote out a cheque of two hundred pounds to the after school club of ESGS. The guests all left for Gatwick airport in the hired coach from where they departed to Nigeria.

Chapter Ten

BATTLE OF LOVE

Upon their return to Nigeria, the parents of the ESGS pupils came for them at Murtala Mohammed international airport on 2nd September 2018. The children were all extremely happy and so noisy on seeing their parents that it was impossible to miss the joys on their parents' faces as they received gifts from their children and Ewaoluwa. They all thanked her and took the children home. After a wonderful time in UK, she was ready for her teaching job as well as her mission to revenge. She had no opportunity to get back at Singh Raj because Tiana held him close and made him a vital part of the program. Though she tried to hint her of what he said, she told her not to worry about it.

Ewaoluwa soon began to prepare for the next academic year that would kick off in a forth night. Her staff resumed and joined her in school few days after she returned from her trip. They organised the program and events for ESGS and got all supplies necessary for a smooth academic run. Almost three weeks afterwards, phone rang. It was Khatumu, the Nigerian senate president.

Now Ewaoluwa had to make up her mind if she could really afford to be his fourth wife and live in the same house with Khadijah and Shamshudeen. However the image of a fallen Dr Oluiferiwa and Ilemobola beclouded her judgement. There was an internal battle for her to live a life of love but it was silently marred by hate. Khatumu asked her out again in Nigeria. This time they visited The Heights restaurant and bar for a Chinese meal. They both ordered rice and duck tongues with assorted vegetables and drank a glass of cognac each. In his characteristic romantic style, he gave her a gift and a bouquet of chrysanthemum flowers. On opening it, she saw a bottle of Aramis perfume. She also gave him a tie and handkerchief set. They exchanged a kiss and as they sat down to eat, they both mused over their holidays in UK. Khatumu said that he thanked God that he met her. Prior to meeting her, he said he always felt depressed in September after his annual feast as all his wives would be with their children; leaving him alone with his domestic staff at home. They then spoke extensively about their expectations from each other in the present relationship; they also discussed their ambitions, visions and political goals.

This time, she was silent on her revenge on Oluiferiwa. She had learnt a lesson from Singh Raj. She would not to discuss her mission with him nor his family, no matter how close or sympathetic they were. She had lost Singh when she told him of her mission to destroy Oluiferiwa. Though she couldn't get rid of Singh on her last trip, she was confident that by her next trip, she would get rid of him. She had more than a year to plan for that.

On her forty first birthday, Khatumu proposed to her and she accepted joyfully. Talking about his fears, he was worried that Ewaoluwa may not want to share his main house with Khadija and Shamshudeen. Ewaoluwa agreed that it might be an issue being an educated christian from a medium class family. She then suggested that they retained the upper flat she shared with her late mother but he reassured her that he had a way round it. He told her that she could live in the three bedroom chalet that was attached to the right wing of his main house at Lekki. He stated that the main house had two wings attached to it; the right and left wing. At the moment, Zubaydah and Fa'iqah shared a wing each with their children but he would ask them to relinquish the right wing to Ewaoluwa. This was because they only occupied the wings when they came round in August every year. Ewaoluwa would be living there all year round with any child she has after her marriage to Khatumu. She was pleased on hearing that and responded that she would be glad to move into the right wing of his house after they got married.

Shortly after Khatumu proposed to Ewaoluwa, he visited her father and sisters in Abuja and bought gifts for them. He then asked for Ewaoluwa's hand in marriage. The engagement was held in Temidire's Kuje residence in Abuja. Her sisters were both present with their families and few friends. That was the first time the Tolulope family met to have a joyful gathering in a long while. The last time they had gathered was at Singh Ghandi's funeral. Ewaoluwa then moved into Khatumu's Leki residence. She soon discovered that both Khadija and Shamshudeen were very humble and quiet. They welcomed her and went about their usual business. Khatumu had domestic staff that ministered to all Ewaoluwa's domestic needs and all she needed to do was concentrate on running her school and supporting her husband.

However Shamshudeen developed a liking for Ewaoluwa because of her political aspirations. She provided the bedrock on which he could penetrate the feminine world easily. His mother, Khadija was very laid back in politics. All he got from her were good, moral and upright home training and academic education. Though an educated and trained teacher, she was allowed to teach only Shamshudeen at home. The times she was out of the Leki residence, she was in Abuja, monitoring his movement from the house they had lived when Khatumu worked in the ministry in Abuja. Khatumu had given the house to Khadijah and her son. She lived there during her son's school terms and both of them lived there during the short term holidays. However they both spent the long term holidays and muslim festivals in his Leki residence. The period they were away from the Leki residence were blissful periods as Ewaoluwa found absolute privacy and had Khatumu's full attention.

In the next one year, with Khatumu's help, Ewaoluwa brought the number of classes in ESGS from year three to year six. They now had to use the entire building for ESGS. She employed more teachers and equipped them to boost the standards of the school. She brought her administrator and another teacher up to speed to help with the running of ESGS and hold forth while she concentrated on building her political profile. Khatumu also inspired her to be a youth counsellor, and set up teams to go round schools in Nigeria to campaign against drug and alcohol abuse. Her greatest penetration was in Shamshudeen's boarding school; Abuja Preparatory College. That was the school the wealthiest Nigerians sent their children. The senior students in the school were notorious for drug dealing during their social outing days, which was why Khatumu made Khadija seat with

Shamshudeen and monitor his movement and activities.

In addition to Khadijah's presence in Shamshudeen's academic life in Abuja, Ewaoluwa also hired him and his friends to be her representatives in the school. The principal was so impressed with her youth program that she allowed them campaign against drug abuse during their social hours in school. On their outing days, they were allowed to raise the awareness in other private schools in Abuja. Khadijah welcomed the program because she knew it would keep her son busy and out of mischief.

More so, at the grass root level, Ewaoluwa used the support from her father and sisters' contacts to run an empowerment program to encourage and support rural women in politics. This endeared her to many in the society. No longer did the women at grassroots level have to watch their husband in politics, they also participate in supporting their husbands as they in turn supported those above them. Thus every woman became a teacher and a mentor, from the grass root to the elite class. Khatumu was really impressed with her zeal and commitment to see projects through to completion. He knew these were assets he would cherish if he got elected as the president of the Federal Republic of Nigeria. The success of the children's exchange program in UK also gained publicity and a lot of parents indicated their interest in supporting her in subsequent trips.

As the election approached, both Khatumu and Ewaoluwa became very busy working in the same political party and campaigning for the seat of the presidency. Her over powering personality turned up again and she became overbearing even in the home. Khatumu sometimes got jealous and was often tempted to compete with her and contest against her. He had to constantly remind himself that they were in the same team, any time he caught himself off guard.

Ewaoluwa had assumed a vital position in the political party; all that was left was for her to get Oluiferiwa on board and execute her revenge. She decided to run another program within the health sector which would include a forceful strategy that would influence the promotion of Dr Oluiferiwa, so he can be in charge at the ministry of health. Her plan was to place political foes under him in strategic positions to frustrate and implicate him out of the office and practice. She thus diverted all her energy to the health program she set up. She began to oversee the health program in all the states, trying to identify the men she could use.

Unknown to her, her relationship with Khatumu was being strained as she battled to balance the love she had for him with the hatred she felt for Dr Oluiferiwa. Since she was planning

LOVE ON SEPARATE GROUNDS

this dastardly act alone, she didn't notice it had also created a rift in her relationship with the people around her. Khadijah and Shamshudeen soon called Khatumu's attention to Ewaoluwa's change of attitude to the family. He promised to do his own private investigation to see what was responsible for her neglectful attitude and obsessive passion for the health program.

On the political front, she had ensured that she met the professional and financial expectations of her party members. She had also positioned people in charge of her other political programs. The only program she concentrated her personal effort on was the one in the health sector. Everyone around her knew of her obsession for the health program and felt she had a genuine passion for the health sector in Nigeria. She was given a lot of accolades and recognition from people all over the country too. Her political party members also told her that they were convinced that she was called into the health sector not education. She often smiled when they made such comments; little did they know that the passion was fuelled by her desire to confront and destroy her former lover.

Few weeks before the elections, Khatumu was in his office when he got a call from the hospital that Ewaoluwa had collapsed due to exhaustion. She had been revived but would be placed under observation. She became well and fit to return home a week later after being place on drips and other medications. Khatumu quietly arranged with the doctors to keep her hospitalised for another week to allow her gain sufficient rest. She had been working tirelessly on her health program around the country.

When Ewaoluwa felt strong enough, she asked to be discharged so that she can continue with her work. The doctors refused to discharge her and she threw a fierce fight in the ward. She threatened to sue them, put them out of jobs and shut down the hospital. She accused them of being incompetent and uncaring. She tried to leave forcefully but was held back by the guards that Khatumu had positioned by the ward to keep an eye on her. She then threatened to destroy all the hospital equipments and create disturbance for all the other patients in the wards.

The hospital staff placed a call and before long Khatumu walked in and she calmed down. He wanted an explanation from Ewaoluwa on why she felt she had to pick a fight with the doctors and threaten them for looking after her interest. She really wanted this sweet revenge but Khatumu looked like an obstacle she had to overcome at all cost. Then she cautioned herself, as she remembered the event that led to her split with Dr Oluiferiwa. Suddenly she resigned to fate, threw caution in the air and broke down crying. She explained that she had to get back at Oluiferiwa and his family for all the hurt and embarrassment they had caused her.

LOVE ON SEPARATE GROUNDS

Khatumu responded in shock 'You mean you agreed to marry me to get back at your old lover, Ewaar'? Khatumu couldn't believe what he was hearing. He was confused and began to panick. As he broke out in sweat, he began to see Ewaoluwa in a different light. He comported himself and braced up to the moment. He couldn't believe that after all the love and affection he showered on her, all he got back was the venom in her. How could a lady that had everything going perfectly well for her be so full of hatred? She only wanted him to get back at her lover. She did all she did to destroy another human being. The deception was too great for him to control himself. He shouted 'Is your head alright, Ewaar, are you insane'? He became very embittered.

Here he was thinking he had finally found the love of his life; the one he would give his very best to. The one that he would take to the president's villa, rule and reign with. The one he would be with till he breathe his last breathe. The academician and a lover of health. She had deceived him into marrying her to get back at a man who didn't even care! He was deeply disappointed. Khatumu ordered her not to move an inch close to his home as he was not prepared to have her there. He promised to hand her body over to his village reptiles for dinner if he sensed her presence anywhere near his Leki residence. He reminded her that his father was a snake charmer and the capital punishment for anyone caught in the act of witchcraft and sorcery in his village was to hand them over to the reptiles in the river, to be eaten alive. He then stormed out of the ward and headed home downcast.

Ewaoluwa then became very scared and had to listen to the doctors who had advised her to stay behind in the ward. A week later, Khatumu paid for her hospital bills and sent the driver to get her. On arrival at their Leki residence, Ewaoluwa found out that all her things had been packed into suitcases and left in the living of the main house. The doors to her chalet were all shut. She burst into tears as Khatumu walked in. She knelt down and began to appeal to him to reconsider and allow her to stay. She said she was badly hurt and he was her only hope of ever getting back at Dr Oluiferiwa.

Khatumu was enraged and said 'Now I am sure a spell has been cast on you'. He left the room for few minutes. On his return, a steward followed him. The steward walked towards Ewaoluwa and poured a bowl of very cold water on her head. She screamed on her knees as she wept and begged him to forgive her. He barked at her and said 'Are you awake now, Ewaar, what did you just say'? She said that she meant that he was the only hope she had in regaining a steady life. She assured him that she loved him and did what she did to prove her love to him. He was disgusted.

How could she bring herself that low? She had stooped so low that he had lost confidence in her and her motives. He then threatened her with divorce, saying he had the mind to order the driver to take her and her belongings back to her school premise where Dr Oluiferiwa had dumped her. She continued to weep and pleaded with him on her knees. He then gave her the conditions under which he would reconsider marriage to her.

Firstly, he told her that he would back down from the election campaign and desire to run for the presidency. She wept further and became hysterical telling him not to dare. He called in the driver and asked her if she was prepared to return to ESGS premise in Surulere. She calmed down. Next he said that she must drop all the political programs she started and hand them over to other party members. She wailed profusely. He whispered to the driver's ears and he picked her up and bundled her into the van. The security men then loaded the vehicle with all her things.

Then Khatumu came to the van to meet her, as she further pleaded with him. He bent over to her in the van and whispered into her ears 'and that is how easy and quick it would be for me to send you back to where you came from Ewaar, do you understand'? She remained silent. He then roared loudly 'Do you understand me, silly', I said do you understand me'? She nodded. 'Good, listen and listen good, silly bitch', he said in disgust. He then told her that if she still wanted to be his wife, all she would be allowed to do is to run ESGS. She must change her life and guard her heart or get divorced and leave his life.

Ewaoluwa looked around her and noticed that she was still in the van. Swallowing her tears, she nodded and grudgingly agreed. She reasoned that her marriage was worth the fight, so she had to forget all about the revenge on Singh Raj and Dr Oluiferiwa. Khatumu then ordered the domestic staff to help her settle down in her chalet. From then onwards he increased the security around her and positioned a body guard to monitor her every move, even in ESGS.

On hearing that his father and Ewaoluwa had pulled out of politics, Shamshudeen became sad. They had agreed that they would be silent over the matter, so Shamshudeen didn't have any clue of what led to the decision. Khatumu told his political party that he didn't think they were the right candidate for the present election. He also allured to the fact that Ewaoluwa recently had a near breakdown and he preferred they bow out now than be sorry.

He ordered Ewaoluwa to join him in a conference meeting he called to bid his political party farewell. He promised her that if she pulled a fast one on him, he would disgrace her publicly by exposing her dark secrets and would make sure she is destroyed completely. He also promised her that if she made the mistake to take him for a fool during the conference or if she moved near politics in the near future, she wouldn't be counted among the living. That was the first time Ewaoluwa saw a man vent his full anger on her. She quivered, even Dr Oluiferiwa hadn't been that violent.

However Shamshudeen on the other hand soon got over his father's decision for the family to pull out of the elections. He was told that it was alright for him to continue without them. Having made enough contacts, he continued with his political pursuits since most of Khatumu's political party members were people he knew very well. The only difference then was that he had to submit to the leadership of those other than his parents. He then aspired to be a member of the house of representative.

Meanwhile, Khatumu and Khadija guided Ewaoluwa back into the acceptable family life, devoid of politics. She now had to submit to Khadijah in the house. The trustees in ESGS also increased their level of commitment to ensure that she did the right thing always. At the elections, the political party which Khatumu and Ewaoluwa set up won but they had pulled out, so another political aspirant was elected as president of the Federal Republic of Nigeria.

On hearing the news, it was the worst pain Ewaoluwa had ever experienced. She didn't believe her luck. She had worked tirelessly for a position that someone else just walked in to fill. When she heard the results, she didn't know which pain was worse; the one caused by Dr Oluiferiwa initially or the one caused by Khatumu when he forced them out of the elections. She then had to consider if she was going to carry out revenge on Dr Oluiferiwa, Singh Raj and Khatumu. Though sad and dejected, she muttered to herself 'Ewaar, you are ridiculously insane'. She wept silently for many days, knowing she had been given a choice to love or to hate. She chose to love after many nights of silent personal internal battles. She must let go and move on at all cost or she would lose all.

Although Khatumu felt bad at the results, he was happy that his son was elected as a member of the house of representative in Abuja. The interesting thing was that Shamshudeen was just in his first year in University of Abuja, pursuing a degree in political science. He had learnt a lot from the Khatumu, Khadijah and Ewaoluwa to live a balanced life. He had turned out to be a fine gentle man, full of wisdom and intelligence. He was very smart, tall and dark complexion like his father. The election result taught Khatumu to continue his business but keep his political life away from Ewaoluwa and Khadijah.

Later on Ewaoluwa settled down to her work as the head teacher in her school. It was soon time to plan for another teachers' exchange program with Sanderstead Tiny Feet. Ewaoluwa wasn't allowed to attend the teachers' exchange program but ESGS children were allowed to attend the children's exchange program initiated by Ewaoluwa. This time, they had thirty ESGS pupils from year one to year six showing interest in going. They were to be accompanied by five ESGS teachers, their administrator and Ewaoluwa.

The Freeman Cottage could not accommodate all of them so they liased with the Littlewoods and Tiana. They booked all the fifty rooms in Croham Park bed and breakfast for the week long program. A bigger coach would be hired for the whole week to take them on their outings. As the final preparations for the trip was being prepared, Ewaoluwa collapsed again in her office and was rushed to the hospital.

Report later got to Khatumu who on getting to the hospital was told that Ewaoluwa was expecting a baby. He was overjoyed. That would bring the number of his children to ten. It meant that while Shamshudeen was at the university, he would have another child at home. Ewaoluwa was well enough to take ESGS pupils for their exchange program and it was been a huge success.

A couple of months after Ewaoluwa returned from the children's exchange program in UK, she was delivered of a set of twin baby girls. She named them Oluwatunmininu (God comforted me) and Morireoluwa (I saw the goodness of God). Khatumu gave Oluwatunmininu the name Na'imah (meaning enjoying the bounty of God) and he gave Morireoluwa the name Samirah (meaning jovial companion). At forty two years old, a set of twins had turned up in Ewaoluwa's life and she had found the true love she had searched for all her life, after stepping on different grounds. The scars of the past life as a fighter and loser in love began to fade away gradually as she faced her new life as a mother and a wife.

Walking through the gallery of love, Ewaoluwa had discovered what true love was. Who could have thought that the ordeal she had to fight for over twenty years would end in bliss and she would bounce back strong after Singh Ghandi's demise? As she saw her baby girls, she felt so sorry for the life that she had lived. She felt so sorry for her baby girls and hope they never have to experience such a life. Suddenly executing revenge on Dr Oluiferiwa, Singh Raj or Khatumu felt very nauseating.

She didn't believe she had let the cat out of the bag with Khatumu. Actually she felt he would be happy and use his influence to support her and teach Dr Oluiferiwa a lesson. She was so wrong. The only partner that she successfully discussed her mission with was Alfred Costcutter. He listened to her and also threw his weight behind her to ensure she accomplished it. That came at a huge cost; she paid with her body for several nights. She was fortunate that Alfred had other sleeping mates. He allowed her walk away without causing any drama, after the several nights she spent with him in bed. Thinking back now, she had regrets for the price she paid. She felt so ashamed thinking about her past and only hoped Alfred would be kind enough to keep his mouth shut permanently. Only the mercy of God would keep her out of the police custody if he dared opened his mouth.

The cries of the twins soon brought her back to real time. The love she felt as she carried and fed the babies in turn compensated for all the loses. She only prayed that the shame of the past that was beginning to creep into her future would go away with time. God had really prevented her from being found out and disgraced on many occasions. She was glad that she was now married and had her own children. This was a guarantee that she would not be going back to look for Alfred Costcutter again. She would also be far from Boogie Afrikana and her highly influential friends that dealt with drugs too. Ewaoluwa now understood her own mother's testimony. Like her late mother, Temiloluwa, God was there all along endowing her with love, protecting and delivering her from evil, yet she didn't know it. God was with her from her youth where she had outstanding performances right through to her marriage to Khatumu and the birth of the baby girls. All that was lost had been found, from her first marriage to her teaching career.

More so, her sisters that once thought all hope was lost on her had repented, and once again, she was a force to be reckoned with. She had also regained the love of her friends who had stood with her, even when they didn't need to. Her previous disappointing records hadn't deterred them. Despite her adamant attitude to revenge at all cost, love found her as she stepped on different grounds, going into relationships for all the wrong reasons.

She then said to Khatumu 'It pains to walk away from a sweet revenge, it really hurts the soul'. Khatumu's response was 'oh no dear, do not go there again. We are done with that now, backward never darling. Look what the Lord had done'. She then said, 'I know, babes. In the gallery of love, winners take all; finance, fame, friends and foe. Losers descend the stairs with each passing second. Play to win, not one but all'.

To which he replied 'Very accurate my dear, to win this game of love, and live and walk in it, you must equip your feet with the sandal of love, guard your heart with the breastplate of love, protect your loins with the belt of love, put on the helmet of love, take up the shield of love before grabbing your sword of love. Then under the

LOVE ON SEPARATE GROUNDS

banner of love, you can pass the baton of love to others as you win the battle of love with all your acts of love. You must shun all forms of hatred and make love your aim. You must let go of all hurts and make love a priority. You must forgive and forget and make love your value.

About The Author

Christiana .T. Moronfolu is firstly an aspiring architect then an author. She had her training at Yaba College of Technology (2000) before proceeding to London South Bank University (2013). She later had her masters in Construction Project Management from same university (2015). While on career breaks, she diverts her energy to private studies and also writing. She has added two novels, 'Pansy's Chest' (2018) and 'Love On Seperate Grounds' (2018) to her existing collections; Destiny's Garden (2012) and Destiny's Fight (2012). Through her writings, she hopes to inspire, inform, entertain, admonish, encourage and celebrate her readers.